Sept. 17, 2012

Dear Inez + Frank

Thank you for your
kind Friendship

Con affetto
Nora Menotti
Agostoni

The Stolen Masterpiece

Nora Agostini

authorHOUSE®

AuthorHouse™
1663 Liberty Drive
Bloomington, IN 47403
www.authorhouse.com
Phone: 1-800-839-8640

This book is a work of fiction. Names, characters, places and incidents are a product of the author's imagination and are used fictitiously . Any resemblance to an actual event or persons dead or living is coincidental.

Published by AuthorHouse 2/7/2012

ISBN: 978-1-4670-2620-8 (sc)
ISBN: 978-1-4670-2619-2 (e)

Library of Congress Control Number: 2011916127

}{for "The Stolen Masterpiece (75349) } T

This book is printed on acid-free paper.

This book is dedicated to my beloved parents
Louisa & Leopoldo Menotti, my husband Fabio,
our children and our delightful grandchildren.

ACKNOWLEDGEMENTS

I express my deepest gratitude to my husband, Fabio, my children Mary, Joe, Jeanne and Stephen and their wonderful families, for giving me many blessings in my lifetime.

Thanks, Jeanne Melendez, my daughter for editing my manuscript, and for allowing me to understand the profession of a lawyer, better.

Special thanks to my kind proofreaders, Lois Rycx , and my generous typing preparer, Ada Zambanini.

My appreciation goes out to my nursing buddies, Noreen and Maureen for sharing their nursing skills.

A large thank you goes to the members of the Club Trentino of NYC. New York, as they proudly provided me with the cultural and culinary traditions of the Tyrolean-Trentino area of Italy.

To Nassau Community College, Toby Bird PhD. class on autobiographical writing and her informative students, I thank you all, for not only improving my writing skills, but for making it fun.

To all mystery book fans, keep on enjoying the fun in solving the mystery.

Author's Note

The painting, "The Annunciation," the small replica of the masterpiece by Leonardo da Vinci doesn't exist. The author took literary license to invent the painting and its owner in this work of fiction.

The author respectfully advises all who visit Florence, Italy to view the original masterpiece of da Vinci's "Annunciation" at the Uffizi Galleria.

THE STOLEN MASTERPIECE

As the thunderous August rainstorm subsided, Tony Pacelli hails a cab outside of his Manhattan apartment to attend his retirement dinner from the NYC police department, at La Fortuna Restaurant in Greenwich Village. He has just completed his 21st year on the police force. As this tall slender man with sandy blonde hair and sad blue eyes enters the Italian bistro, many memories flood his mind.

Shortly after his graduation from John Jay College, Tony remembers receiving his acceptance to the NYC police department. Coming from a family of police officers he recalls that letter which brought his memory back to his father who lost his life protecting a woman during a domestic dispute. While Tony cherishes the thought of his father as a hero, his mind constantly questions his own courage.

He needs to overcome his fear of not being able to protect the public, against his desire to possess the strong emotion of altruism. Besides these conflicts, he carries a deeper secret, his fear of dying on the job like his father.

Accepting his police assignments his life goes along like a tidal wave. He climbs the ranks to detective during his twenty years on the police force through community service and written tests. On the tenth year on the force, Tony is feeling confident; it's this same year that he meets Maria Simone. He can't believe his luck when his heart flips for this 27 year old woman with light brown hair and glistening green eyes, a newly appointed assistant D.A.

Maria's love makes him strong. He begins to relax more with his police work. As a mature thirty-two year old man, he feels complete love, and is ready for a commitment. Maria and Tony enjoy each other's company; mostly they just always want to be together. Unfortunately, the following year comes upon them as a huge black cloud. Maria is continually feeling fatigued, so she goes to the doctor. The physician tests her to the maximum with laboratory tests. Finally, she's diagnosed with acute lymphoblastic leukemia. That year she endures months of chemotherapy and ultimately receives a bone marrow transplant. Although all methods of treatments are exhausted, Maria succumbs to the disease and dies. Tony's heart sinks to the deepest abyss of darkness. He feels like a cement wall has fallen on his chest. To keep his sanity he devotes his next nine years exclusively to the service of the police department.

Tony is grateful that he has finally reached the end of his police work without being embroiled in any legal situations. Mostly he just wants to enjoy the aftermath of completing satisfactorily his proud professional career.

All these thoughts crowd his mind at the conclusion of his party. He thanks his fellow officers and leaves for his home.

He calls for a taxi and returns to his apartment on 34th Street and 2nd Avenue.

CHAPTER TWO

Before climbing the stairs to his apartment, Tony reflects on how lonely he has been since his beloved Maria's death.

"I must make some changes," he mulls over.

He looks at the mailbox, opens it and collects a huge amount of cards and letters. Most of the mail are wishes for his retirement. As he goes to the second floor, with a huge bundle in his arms, he experiences difficulty unlocking the door. He flings his raincoat over the brown leather sofa and proceeds to drop the cascade of mail on the kitchen table. As the mail drops from the table, Tony notices an air mail letter.

"Ah!" Zia Erna, his aunt in Italy remembered his retirement. With a smile on his face, he opens the letter.

> Caro Tony,
>
> I congratulate you on your retirement; I wish you many years of happiness and adventures. (Zia had lived in the USA so her written English is pretty good).
>
> I do have a favor to ask of you. Over the

last few months we've been having a series of thefts at the hotel. Our guests have had jewelry and money stolen. Although the carabinieri have been summoned, nothing has been solved. I would be deeply grateful, if you could come to Italy and help me.

Con affetto,
Zia Erna

With a tear in his eyes, he remembers how Zia Erna helped him during his large sorrow from Maria's death. He spent a month at her hotel during his deep seated grief. Tony's mind visualizes his kind sixty-year old aunt, although petite in stature, at only five feet two inches, she possesses the courage of a David. He sweetly grins, as he recalls how each morning in Italy, Zia would swiftly spin her silvery wheat colored hair into a bee hive at the back of her head. Mostly, he cherishes her clear hazel eyes which reflect a serenity that could calm the eye of any storm. How could he refuse Zia! He picks up the phone and calls his mother, Zia Erna's older sister.

"Hi! Mom, I just received a letter from Zia Erna".

He proceeds to explain the contents of the letter. She agrees that Tony should travel to Italy to help his aunt.

The next day he arranges his trip to Northern Italy.

CHAPTER THREE

Tony calls his aunt in Italy. She picks up the phone, "Pronto. Ciao Tony. I'm so glad to hear from you. Did you get my letter?"

Tony responds, "Si. I'm sorry that you are having so many problems. I'll be glad to help you with the robbery investigations."

"Good!" Zia Erna answers.

Tony continues, "I'm coming to Italy this Saturday around two o'clock in the afternoon."

Zia asks if he needs to be picked up at the airport. "No, grazie, there's no need as I'm renting a car at the Marco Polo Venice airport. Ciao Zia. See you Saturday."

Zia puts down the phone, takes off her apron, changes into her walking shoes and crosses the street to her hotel.

It's early afternoon, the guests are finishing their lunch. The staff's scurrying around clearing the dining room tables.

Zia Erna enters the manager's office. Marco Zini, the hotel manager of the II Bel Fior Hotel, jumps up to greet his aunt.

"Ciao, Zia."

This tall slim forty-year old man stands rigidly in his usual dark suit and tie. He spends most of his day in his office organizing future trips for new and previous clients. His light brown eyes wander around his office before he continues to speak with his aunt. "Zia, can I assist you?"

"Si, I just came over to tell you that Tony is coming this Saturday."

"Vacation?"

"No." Zia replies. "I asked him to come to help us with the investigation of these hotel thefts."

Marco's brother Mirro looks over at Zia. Overhearing something about Tony, he comes quickly running over to their side.

Mirro is the maître di of the hotel. He is in his forties, medium built, with searching brown eyes and quick feet. As he enters a room he always seems ready to perform.

He is well liked by the hotel guests because he enjoys joking with the vacationers. Also, he rejoices in staying up late with the customers for late night drinking and card playing. He can since he is the only unmarried hotel working brother.

But rumors are murmuring at the hotel that he has gambling problems.

Seeing Mirro go over to Zia, the two other brothers come out of the kitchen. They are the hotel chefs with many years of culinary experience. Mario, the oldest brother, is tall and handsome with a bronze complexion and curly brown hair; he resembles a model posing for a sculpture at a Florentine studio. He speaks very little but when he does his brothers listen.

The youngest brother Gianni is in his thirties. He is the tallest one, around six foot three. His fair complexion and his smiling clear blue eyes gleam whenever he receives his prizes as a renowned pastry genius.

They stand there listening to Marco as he discusses excitedly about the thievery that has occurred at the hotel.

Mirro stares at Zia and exclaims in a high pitched tone,

"Why did you bother Tony? We can handle the theft problems ourselves with the insurance company."

Zia responds in a soft tone, "I think we need Tony's experience since he has been a detective on the New York City police force for over twenty years."

Please set aside a room for Tony this Saturday, Zia advises gently.

She leaves and goes into the corridor looking for Angelica. Zia sees a tall slender woman in her thirties, with brown hair and serious brown eyes, who is coming out of one of the rooms.

Zia calls to her, "Angelica."

This young lady locks the door and walks quickly over to her aunt.

"Buon giorno! Angelica. I've come to tell you that Tony is arriving here, on Saturday."

Angelica smiles broadly as she admires Tony.

"Good. I'll get his room ready."

Zia hugs and thanks her. Angelica is the one who is in charge of the rooms. She's a quiet person but takes optimum care of the hotel guests.

Zia appreciates all her nephews' and her niece's help, as she has no children. They are the ones who kept the hotel going after the death of her husband Beppi, four years ago. Her husband Beppi was their uncle, only through Zia's marriage. They are the children of Zia Erna's brother.

The aunt leaves to water the hanging crimson red ivy geraniums that surround the upper balcony of her chalet hotel. This structure has a grandiose background of the majestic Italian Alps, in particular the Paganella.

This mountain is the most colorful in the Italian Alps. In the summer, the Paganella Mountain glistens with tiny spots of yellow, lavender and royal blue bell flowers sticking their heads out of the mountain's wet snow. The most treasured flower which nestles on the side of the Alpine mountains is the velvet shiny ones. This flower's white pointy velour textured petals surround its puffy yellow tinged center. It appears like it has been kissed by the sun. To the Italians it is known as the Stella Alpina, while to the Austrians it is called the Edelweiss. This is one of the reasons that the vacationers flock to this region.

In the hotel, Marco takes his three brothers and his sister Angelica back to his office to talk with them. The first to speak is Mirro. He doesn't want to listen to anyone.

He babbles in a fiery tone, "That meddling old lady. Tony has no right to know our hotel business."

"Merda!" He starts cursing. With a wave of his hand he begins to leave.

Angelica critically reprimands him. "Be quiet Mirro. Maybe Tony can help us." Mirro shakes his hand and points his middle finger demonstratively to the group. They all disperse to go about their hotel duties.

CHAPTER FOUR

Friday arrives. Tony makes quite a presence. His tall lean stature and his soft smiling Roman face frames a person who makes strangers feel comfortable. He packs his suitcase and his backpack; he is ready for his trip to Italy. He calls his mother to set up arrangements with her to oversee his apartment and to collect his mail.

"Hi Mom! Just calling to ask you to look in on my apartment, while I'm in Italy."

"Of course, Tony. Take all the time you need."

"I took care of all my bills," Tony tells her.

"Ciao. Have a good end of the summer, and thank you! Thanks for helping my sister. Have a safe trip," his mother responds.

Tony puts down the phone.

He picks up his suitcase and jacket, and gets ready to leave for his trip. He calls the taxi service for a 5:00 pm pickup to take him to New York City's JF Kennedy Airport. The taxi arrives on time to take him immediately to the airport. Arriving at the airport Tony proceeds to get his boarding pass. Happily, he has a half hour to relax before boarding his flight.

As the time approaches he climbs into the 747 international jet plane; the pilot announces that the trip to Venice, Italy will take approximately eight hours. He finds his seat and gets himself comfortable. The meal is served at the beginning of the flight, which makes Tony happy. After finishing his meal with a glass of red wine, he curls up and puts himself in a harmonious position where he falls asleep for five hours.

When he wakes up the flight attendants are preparing the passengers for a light breakfast. The plane lands on time, Saturday 9:30 am. Tony collects his luggage and proceeds to Avis to pick up his rental car.

Unfortunately, they do not have an automatic car available, so they give him a semi-automatic one. Tony agrees.

He enters the vehicle and attempts to start it. It bucks and stalls out. Tony waves to the attendant. The young man rushes over and instructs Tony on how to work the gears to facilitate his driving. Quickly, Tony grasps the instructions.

Tony is on his way for his three hour trip to the Val'D'Adige region in northern Italy. Procuring some bottles of water and a prosciutto panino, he commences his trip on the autostrada to his aunt's hotel, II Bel Fior.

CHAPTER FIVE

A little after one p.m. he arrives at the front door of the hotel. The hotel is alive with the sound of dishes and the chatter of the guests.

Angelica notices Tony right away. She swiftly runs to the door to greet him. With a strong embrace she welcomes him. Marco, the manager, greets Tony politely and assists him to his room on the second floor. Tony puts his bags on the floor of his room. Then he decides to shower and change his clothes before going to his aunt's house. Finally, he looks into his knapsack and pulls out Estee Lauder's White Linen eau de toilette. He bought it at the airport especially for her, as it is her favorite fragrance.

Feeling refreshed, he descends down the back of the hotel and crosses the street to his aunt's house. There he presents her with his gift.

In the comfort of Zia's kitchen, Tony sits for over two hours simply enjoying Zia's homemade gnocchi, veal cutlets and a plentiful garden salad. After finishing his meal, with a frothy cappuccino in his hand, he relaxes into a comfortable discourse with his aunt regarding the hotel thefts. He tells her that he will get a better view of the problems in the next coming days.

As the evening approaches, Tony decides to take a short walk around the center of the town. He notices that the cafes and restaurants are crowded and busy with many vacationers. Feeling tired he calls it a day. He returns to the hotel, climbs up to the second floor, making a mental note to get up early the next day to meet the guests at the hotel.

CHAPTER SIX

Tony sets his alarm for 6:30 am the next morning. He plans to meet all the guests at the hotel. The shrills of the alarm clock wakes Tony immediately. He showers, puts on his blue Izod sport shirt and his khaki long pants and walks down to the breakfast area.

Seeing Angelica briskly serving the early guests their coffee, Tony calls to his cousin,

"Ciao Bella!" She smiles and tells him to help himself to some panini and coffee. Angelica has set out on a long table in the foyer, an assortment of rolls, fresh fruits and yogurts. The guests can go to the table to choose their own foods. Angelica places a carafe of hot coffee, warm milk, butter and jams at each table prepared for four.

All of a sudden, like the wind blowing from the front door, in comes a long-legged, lovely twenty-year old woman. She has hair of golden honey color and her presence startles the room with her sparkling azure eyes.

She goes to Angelica. "Scusa, I overslept." She grabs a hotel apron and immediately starts to arrange the tables for the new guests who are arriving for breakfast.

Angelica calls to her. "Come, I want you to meet Tony, my cousin from New York."

"Tony, this is Mirella, a student from the University of Trento. She is working at the hotel for the summer months."

Mirella charmingly smiles at Tony.

"It's a great pleasure." She exclaims.

Since she is studying English at the University of Trento, this is a great opportunity for her to use the language.

Tony reflects that she is quite a vision to behold.

With a strong thrust of the door, in comes Mirro, the jovial maitre d'. He screens the room. First he compliments the ladies, and then he jokes with the children. All of a sudden his face blushes seeing the waitress, Mirella.

Moving to her side, he greets her, "Ciao carina!"

She tilts her head, flashing him a coy smile.

Tony enters the dining room and waves to his cousin, Mirro.

Tony observes all the guests in the dining room. He goes to speak to an older couple seated in the corner of the room. "What healthy looking octogenarians!" Tony assesses. He takes his coffee to their table and introduces himself.

"Buon giorno!" He speaks to them in Italian. "Io sono Tony Pacelli di New York."

The older gentleman extends his hand to Tony. "Piacere. Io sono Paolo Montagni e questa e la mia moglie, Maria."

The husband informs Tony that he is a retired plumber from Milan. His wife states that for these past ten years they have been vacationing in the Trentino region because of its beautiful mountains and delicious cuisine.

Tony surmises that they seem like a pleasant couple. After a short conversation, they pick up their backpack and leave for a hike near the mountains. They give Tony a fond farewell.

Tony turns around and sees an older woman arriving with a young lady in her thirties. The gray haired woman is neatly dressed in a navy blue tailored suit. Although she appears to be in her seventies, she stands with good posture. Tony admires her face, as pleasant with very few wrinkles. The young woman is of average height with long light chestnut colored hair and sparkling green eyes. Tony experiences a tingling sensation through his body when she smiles. He slowly walks over to their table, and introduces himself. He asks permission to sit down. The young woman introduces him to her aunt.

"This is my aunt, Silvia Bonetti." Then she says, "I'm Gabriella Longhi."

"We both live in a town outside of Firenze." Gabriella adds, "I can speak in English. I studied for many years."

"Good. That will make it easier for me." Tony responds.

Tony tells them about himself, his retirement, and his vacation with his aunt, the owner of the hotel. Sitting comfortably with these guests, Gabriella mentions that she is an assistant curator at the Uffizi Galleria in Florence.

She explains that she is staying at the hotel to experience the great art work that Signora de' Medici is loaning to the museum in Trento. This long standing de' Medici treasure, a smaller painting of the Leonardo da Vinci's "Annunciation," is a masterpiece held by the de' Medici family for many centuries. This loan to the museum is considered the most grandiose moment in the Art world.

Tony enjoys talking to these ladies, especially the young woman, but he must go and chat with other guests. He gets up, says his "Ciao" and continues speaking to the other families staying at the hotel. The rest of the guests are mostly middle-aged parents with teenage children.

Tony doesn't stay long with them. He says his cordial good-byes and crosses the street to his Zia Erna's house.

CHAPTER SEVEN

Tony finds Zia Erna, as she is sweeping the terrace of her apartment. She stops and smiles broadly at her nephew.

"Zia, I've come to speak with you about the carabinere and the insurance company that's involved in this theft case."

Zia opens the door to her apartment. Tony and his aunt enter the kitchen and sit by her circular pinewood table.

"Tony, the Alto Adige Insurance Company is handling the requests for compensation for the victims of the hotel burglaries."

"They say that they must investigate the hotel personnel first, then the guests. The agent in charge is Signor Tenalglia. His office is in Bolzano, approximately 50 km from Trento."

"Okay," answers Tony. "I'm writing all these facts down in my little book."

"Now I want to know the name of the carabiniere who is in charge of this case."

"His name is Ispettore Portari, Antonio." Zia continues, "I think you should go to Trento to see him."

"I'll go right now." As he is about to leave, Zia's kitchen door is thrust open and in comes Roberto Scoffo, Angelica's fiancé.

He is a well built muscular man, in his mid-forties, with murky blonde hair and deep blue eyes; he slaps Tony on the back, "Welcome! Tony I'm so glad to see you."

Although he works as an accountant at the Museo di Buon Consiglio in Trento, he enjoys keeping up a macho appearance.

"Still working out",interjects Tony.

Roberto proudly smiles expressing his broad shoulders. Quickly his face changes and he shows his concerns for Zia's hotel thefts. Tony enjoys his company but he doesn't understand why Roberto, after eight years of courtship with his cousin Angelica, he hasn't married her.

Quickly, Tony says his goodbyes.

Entering his car, he takes off for the city of Trento. This is not a large city, but it has all the needed institutions required for quality living. Approaching the town, the first thing he views is a large train station, decorated with large baskets of red geranium and purple petunias surrounding the waiting room.

Proceeding to the main square in the center of the town, Tony sees a gigantic statue of King Neptune with a spear in his hand, which is standing in the midst of an uplifting spurting waterfall. All along the cobblestone streets there are many different stores, ranging from boutiques to hardware shops. Besides, this town has an abundant number of restaurants, most of them with outdoor cafes.

The city of Trento busily spreads out, displaying many tall brick government buildings and historical museums. The Province of Trento is expanding so rapidly and successfully with many lovely new condos and new apartments for the young and the elderly who hope to live there.

Driving his car Tony looks around; he spots a sign CARABINIERI, on a tall red brick building. He parks his vehicle at a timed meter. As he enters the building, Tony asks the desk officer in Italian. "Voglio parlare con il Ispettore." The police officer answers in English. "Are you an American?"

"Si!" answers Tony. "It's important that I see the Inspector."

"Uno momento." The young police officer leaves and goes down the hallway into a room.

Returning, he says, "Okay, the Inspector wants to speak to you on this phone."

Tony picks up the phone. "Pronto," Tony responds.

He tells the Inspector that he is here in Italy to assist his aunt, Erna Zini, in resolving the matter of the thefts at II Bel Fior Hotel.

The Inspector answers, "I'll be right out."

A short, rotund, slightly balding dark haired, middle-aged man with tired blue eyes quietly ambulates out to receive the American.

CHAPTER EIGHT

The Inspector comes into the waiting room. He extends his hand, "I'm Inspector Antonio Portari."

"Piacere and my name is Tony Pacelli." The Inspector continues, "Please come to my office where we can speak in private. I can speak in English. I studied Political Science at Fordham University in New York City, for four years."

Tony keenly observes and follows him.

Although he seems like a friendly man, Tony notices that he has very astute eyes.

"Sit down, do you want some coffee?" Tony replies, "Si, grazie!"

Tony contemplates that the coffee will make for a more relaxing conversation. Tony listens attentively, as the Inspector divulges the facts regarding the theft of gold chains and watches which occurred at II Bel Fior Hotel. Continuing he states, "One evening they even stole a wallet with two thousand euros."

Tony looks up at the Inspector. He informs him that he is a recently retired New York City police detective.

Portari continues with his report. "Even some expensive clothes were pilfered from vacationers' rooms."

Tony suggests, "Although I do not want to get in your way, I'd be happy to help you in any way I can."

The Inspector is an extremely cautious man, but he senses a good feeling with this American.

"Si, I think we can be useful to each other." They shake hands, both say a cheerful goodbye.

As Tony leaves the police building, he sees Gabriella from across the plaza. She's talking to Roberto at the top steps of the Arts museum. The two of them appear to be having a friendly conversation. Tony closes his car door, and places more euros into the timed meter, in order to stay longer in Trento. He calls to Gabriella, and waves to her to come over to him. She crosses the street to Tony. Although she is cordial, she appears a little rigid.

Tony cheerfully asks, "It's lunch time. How about something to eat?"

She agrees. They both enter a nearby trattoria. They sit down and order a salad of prosciutto and cheeses. As they continue talking, the waiter places a carafe of Merlot wine and two glasses on their table. Tony thanks the waiter, as they wait for their food.

Gabriella seems to relax more, she tells Tony that she went to the museum to get more information about the treasured painting that Louisa de' Medici is loaning this week to the museum. Tony listens intensely, as she continues enthusiastically talking about this great acquisition for il Museo di Buon Consiglio. Tony enjoys watching her eyes sparkle when she speaks about renowned paintings and sculptures. When the food comes they both enjoy some good conversation with many smiles and an occasional laugh. Tony realizes how easy it is to speak to this woman.

But he reminds himself that he must proceed with caution. Gabriella suddenly stands up quickly and says, "I must get back to my aunt." She reaches into her handbag for her wallet to pay for her meal. Tony stops her, "It's my treat."

"Grazie for the meal and the company," responds Gabriella. "This has been a pleasure."

"See you at the hotel." Tony sits awhile pensively disturbed.

Both of them return to their own vehicle, as they leave for their trip back to the hotel.

CHAPTER NINE

There's much scampering and bustling around II Bel Fior Hotel, as they are getting ready for the arrival of Signora Louisa de' Medici and her husband Professore Luigi Leonetti. This is a grand occasion, since they are staying at the hotel as honored guests, requested by the Provincia di Trento. Louisa is known as a descendant of the famous de' Medici family from Florence, Italy.

In the sixteen century, Lorenzo de' Medici a renowned patron of the Arts, had only one child, Anna Maria. Lorenzo was extremely generous with Anna Maria, that he commissioned the renowned Leonardo da Vinci to paint a smaller version of his famous "Annunciation" as a gift for his daughter.

Since Anna Maria had no children, she left a Will stating that any descendent from the de' Medici lineage will be the recipient and holder of the de' Medici possessions. This painting was one of the bequests that was kept only for the family's enjoyment throughout the centuries.

After many centuries of traveling into different de' Medici families, in the 21st century, the famous da Vinci painting, his smaller "Annunciation" is inherited by Louisa de' Medici.

Being a generous patron of the Arts, Louisa decides that this masterpiece should be viewed and enjoyed by the Italian public. She decrees to start its travel by loaning it, first to the Museo di Buon Consiglio in Trento, Italy. She chose this museum because she wants to show her gratitude to this beautiful region of Italy for her happy summers spent in their mountainous terrain during her childhood.

CHAPTER TEN

Professore Luigi Leonetti, Louisa de' Medici's husband from Fiesole, a town near Florence, Italy telephones II Bel Fior Hotel to inform Marco the manager, that they will arrive at the hotel this Saturday around seven in the evening.

With all the talk of the masterpiece, high excitement gives liveliness to the hotel. Tony immediately decides to notify Inspector Portari that the da Vinci masterpiece is coming to the II Bel Fior Hotel this Saturday.

Tony phones Inspector Portari. A police officer picks up the phone. Tony insists that it's important that he speak to the Inspector.

The Inspector picks up his phone. "Pronto, ciao, Signor Pacelli."

Quickly Tony replies, "Please Inspector, call me Tony."

"Bene!" Answers Inspector Portari.

Portari listens to all the information that Tony doles out.

Then the Inspector answers.

"Grazie, I appreciate all your input. I have also been notified by Dottore Franzoi, the museum's direttore regarding the arrival of the smaller "Annunciation" the da Vinci's masterpiece, that's coming to your hotel. Thanks again! I will arrange quietly for plain-clothes carabinieri to be sent to the hotel, to keep surveillance until the masterpiece is received at the Museo di Buon Consiglio. I will come to II Bel Fior Hotel today to check out the hotel."

"See you soon." Inspector informs.

Tony puts away his cell phone. He goes around assessing and trying to be helpful while he's waiting for the Inspector.

Tony pulls his aunt aside and advises her about the Inspector's plan.

"Grazie, Tony. That makes me feel better. I'll relate all the information to Marco."

CHAPTER ELEVEN

The Inspector and his undercover agents surround the Il Bel Fior Hotel in a casual work plan. The hotel's preparations are completed. Now, all that's left is to await the grand arrival of Professore Leonetti and his famous wife, Louisa de' Medici.

The hallways are enhanced with huge urns of colorful flowers. The gold and white lace tablecloths cover each table which provides a seating for six. A stately pot of purple violets stands in the center of each table, as if it's waiting for royalty.

The staff and the chefs are ready to set forth their regional delectable foods.

Zia Erna examines the look of the hotel. She is very pleased by what she sees. As the hotel is almost filled with hotel guests, she circulates and talks with each guest. She advises them that they can have their dinner at five p.m., if they wish to eat early. But most of the guests prefer to partake of their dinner with the famous couple.

The Inspector and his men quietly lounge around this spacious hotel. Tony is pleasantly providing his aunt with a calming environment, occasionally interjecting with a casual joke. His critical eye for assessment, notices that Mirro is more emotional than usual. He and his waiters are hovering around the front door. Tony figures that Mirro wants to make an important first impression.

Finally just passed 7:30 pm, a black stretch limousine parks in front of the hotel. Everyone in the hotel jumps to attention, while some of Mirro's waiters scurry to open the double doors.

Zia goes out to greet the famous couple, extending her hand with a warm welcome. "Benvenuti!"

There's great excitement at the doorway. Mirro and his waiters brush through the door to unpack the limo. They quickly remove the luggage and a large slender black leather briefcase; swiftly they rush the baggage to the couple's elegant spacious room at the end of the first floor.

This distinguish middle-aged couple enter the hotel. La Signora de' Medici is petite in stature with her dark brown hair elegantly coiffed on top of her head, in her tailored cream silk suit, she enters the hotel first. The Professore follows; he's a slender gentleman of medium height with silver white hair and he is sporting a thin silver pencil mustache. In his light beige linen suit, his entrance commands an air of respect.

Suddenly Signora de' Medici starts to look around frantically.

"Where is my luggage?" her face is flushed with worry and high anxiety.

Mirro pleasantly and boastfully steps forward, "Si, Signora de' Medici it's all ready for you in your room."

"Where is my room please, I must go!" La Signora de' Medici gasps nervously.

Mirro responds and he points to the way. "It's at the end of this corridor."

She snatches the key from Mirro's hand; she pushes and chases him away. Quickly, she runs to the room.

CHAPTER TWELVE

Signora Louisa de' Medici swiftly runs to her numbered hotel room on the first floor. She turns the key, switches on the light and locks the door. Louisa quickly pulls onto the bed the large black leather briefcase; she sighs, as she pulls out and examines the masterpiece. While La Signora is putting back the masterpiece into the leather briefcase, from behind the heavy drapes a huge object plummets down on the back of her head. She falls to the floor with a thud.

Quickly the lights are turned off and the window is opened. The large leather briefcase is urgently shoved out of the window.

Swiftly and mysteriously a person edges out of the room's door to the end of the hallway to an awaiting car. With all the noise inside the hotel, the sound of this car is not heard leaving the driveway.

Tony attentively notices that Signora de' Medici is not in their midst. He quickly summons Inspector Portari. They rush and run to la Signora's room where they notice that the door is ajar.

Tony calls "Signora!"

Upon entering the room he immediately goes to Signora

de Medici, who is lying on the floor in a pool of blood. Tony quickly takes a towel to stop the bleeding at the back of her head and continues to check her pulse at the side of her neck. It's there, but weak. The Inspector urgently cellphones for the emergency MD and the ambulance. Then the Inspector immediately shouts to his men on his telefonino, "Secure the hotel, allow NO ONE to leave!"

The Professore comes running into the room, he kneels down by his wife, "Cara I'm here. II dottore is coming. Please, Bella, hold on!"

It takes only a few minutes, the ambulance arrives with the paramedics and an MD. Immediately the doctor assesses all la Signora's needs. The bleeding has subsided, but the pulse is still weak. The pressure dressing at the back of her head is intact, while the cardiac monitor is hooked up to la Signora's chest. The doctor is diligently overseeing the monitor screen for any of her cardiopulmonary needs.

Oxygen via nasal cannula is administered. She is safely and gently lifted onto a gurney, where an IV is placed, in case cardiac drugs are needed to be quickly administered.

In a safe and expert manner La Signora is placed in the ambulance. There la Signora de' Medici remains still unresponsive.

Climbing into the ambulance, Professore Leonetti and Zia Erna accompany Signora de' Medici to the hospital. With the MD at the victim's side, the ambulance disperses in an accelerated speed to the fully awaiting ER at San Giustino Ospedale di Trento.

CHAPTER THIRTEEN

Tony quickly takes out his notebook from his front pocket, while his eyes are checking out la Signora's room. The carabineiri and the Inspector swiftly secure the room and designate it with their yellow tape as a crime scene. The Inspector assembles the guests and the hotel staff in the large dining room to apprise them of this tragic occurrence. Also he advises them that the carabinieri are presently conducting a search of all the rooms and areas in the hotel for the recovery of La Signora's de' Medici's famous masterpiece. All the doors are closed and secured by the carabinieri. The group starts fidgeting and they begin hastily, speaking to each other.

The Inspector stoically looks at the group, "Please stay calm. You will be served your dinner presently. "

"Upon the completion of your meal, my officers and I will return to speak with each family, individually."

The Inspector leaves the dining room and scurries back to the crime scene. There he finds his forensic team gathering all the items and clues related to this crime case.

Immediately, Portari looks on the floor, where La Signora's body had been. He catches sight of a marble bust statue of Julius Caesar stained with blood, lying on its side on the carpet where La Signora had bled.

The Inspector deduces that this is the probable weapon used in this crime. Without contamination the forensic agent carefully puts on his latex gloves and places the statue into a large laboratory container.

In the corner of the room, Tony is standing scribbling vehemently in his notebook. Hearing footsteps nearby, he looks up as the Inspector approaches.

Tony whispers, "This is such an awful occurrence."

"Si!" Says Inspector Portari, "But you can be assured that we will get the person or persons who did this," he replies soberly.

After counseling his men and the forensic team, the Inspector with his carabinieri hurries around the corner into the dining room to bring all the guests and staff of the hotel up to date with this evening's crime. Tony follows behind.

Suddenly, all the chatter and the clanging of dishes, become soundless. The Inspector calmly advises the patronage that the carabinieri and he will question all the guests and the staff who were present, when the crime occurred. He assures them that they will intermingle with them in fairness, but he says severely that he expects their cooperation.

The carabinieri and the Inspector take different sides of the room. After the questioning is completed, each officer gives his complete and copious notes to the Inspector.

Before the Inspector encourages the guests to go to their rooms, he scrutinizes his papers and informs the guests,

"You are to proceed to your same rooms. I will advise you in the morning of your own personal situation. Any questions see me after this talk. If you remember anything that could be useful in this case, please call me on my telefonino. All your statements will be typed and you can review and sign them tomorrow morning."

Quietly, they begin to scatter to their rooms.

The Inspector calls out, "Wait, I need to question the staff further. No one is to leave this hotel tonight, understand?" All the guests continue to their rooms.

Looking firmly at the hotel staff, the Inspector declares, "Marco will make arrangements for you, the staff to have rooms for tonight."

After I question each of the staff, you can go to the manager for your rooms." The Inspector speaks to each hotel worker individually. After a short review, Inspector Portari informs them to go, and get their instructions from Marco, the manager.

Tony goes to the office and makes Zerox copies of his investigation and his notes on this criminal case. He gives the Inspector a copy. Then he informs the Inspector,

"I'm going to the hospital in the early morning."

Inspector replies "Okay, I'll probably see you there." Downheartedly, the Inspector continues, "Tony, the masterpiece was not found. It's gone!" They both leave in silence.

Tony hurries to his room. He showers and puts on his pajama bottoms. Feeling hot, he walks out to his room's terrace to catch his breath and to cool off.

As he stares at the sky and mountains, slowly, his focus lands on the driveway below. Unexpectedly, his gaze settles on two figures, which are closely embracing and kissing. Tony pulls himself into the dark corner of the terrace. He strains to see, "Oh....my....God! Its Mirro and Mirella."

CHAPTER FOURTEEN

Around 5:30 in the morning, after a disturbing night sleep, Tony eases out of the bed. He showers and dresses in his casual sport clothes and slowly descends to the dining area to get his quick espresso and a light breakfast bun. There he sees his cousin Angelica engrossed in thought.

"Come va?" "How's it going?" She's startled by Tony's voice.

She then blurts out to Tony. "I called Roberto last night to tell him about Signora de' Medici's assault and the robbery of the da Vinci masterpiece. I must say that I was disappointed not to see him at the hotel last night. But he did say that he would go to the hospital to assist the Professore in all his needs."

Tony responds in a soft gentle tone, "Oh, he must have had much preparation to accomplish at the museum."

Angelica looks at him, she understands his kindness. Tony turns to her and tells her that he's on his way to the hospital.

Shortly, after a twenty minute drive to Trento, Tony enters the ER, where the nurse informs him that Signora de'

Medici is in the ICU unit. Quickly he enters the elevator, up to the ICU unit.

Two carabinieri are standing by the doorway of the victim's ICU room. Tony nods to the police officers and shows his pass, as he enters the unit to the right. A large room propels into his vision; many technical apparatus are attached to the victim, Louisa. He feels a lump surface in his throat. Since Maria died in the hospital, his tolerance for medical equipment and services makes his stamina weak.

Zia Erna comes to Tony immediately and says, "La Signora is still not responding.

Roberto was helpful last night. He made the arrangements for Signora de' Medici's son and daughter to arrive this morning."

"Good" answers Tony.

Tony goes to console Professore Leonetti. He extends his support.

A couple of hours pass. Tony goes out to the hallway to search for Inspector Portari. He observes two young people who are rushing into the ICU unit. They appear extremely anxious. Tony approaches them, only to find out that they are the adult children of La Signora de' Medici and the Professore. With great empathy he escorts them to their mother's bedside.

"Mama, we're here. It's Anita and Luigi!" They both kiss her on the forehead. Then they sit by her side holding on to her hand.

The nurse is swiftly moving about the patient, inserting medication into the IV tubing. She is continually observing the cardiac monitor for any abnormalities. Her demeanor is constantly of a professional nature. Occasionally, she calmly smiles and puts her hand on the Professore's shoulder.

Close to noontime, the alarm on the cardiac monitor

goes off. The doctors and nurses come running in. "She's in ventricular failure!"

CODE BLUE is called!

The family is gently escorted out of the room. The blinds are drawn, CPR is started.

CHAPTER FIFTEEN

The doctors, nurses and the anesthetists work feverishly inserting the endotracheal tube into Signora de' Medici's throat. The doctor continues swiftly with the chest compression.

Calls for medication, "Adrenalin!" is shouted out and quickly administered by the doctor.

The doctor calls out for an occasional zapping at the victim's chest,

"Stand aside!"

As the doctor shouts out again, he places the pads of the defibrillator on the patient's chest, one more time.

Perspiring, the doctor looks anxiously at the monitor and his staff.

"The Signora is not responding!"

Louisa, the victim, is flat lining on the cardiac monitor.

After working on the patient for another half hour, the flat line on the monitor persists. The cardiologist has to pronounce the time of death at 12:58pm. A sad silence overcomes the emergency staff. The carabinieri take charge and Inspector Portari is quickly alerted.

The cardiologist accepts the job of speaking to the family. He walks out to the Professore and his children.

With a furrowed brow, he places his hand gently on the Professore's shoulder, and whispers,

"I'm so sorry. We could not help your wife."

The son and daughter embrace their sobbing father. The ICU nurse and a priest come into the scene to comfort the family. After the nurses prepare Signora de' Medici for the family's viewing, the group goes to the victim's side. The priest says some prayers, and the nurse escorts some of the group out to allow the family to have some time alone with their sorrow. The doctor leaves a prescription of tranquillizers for the family members.

Inspector Portari arrives and secures the hospital room. He takes charge of La Signora Louisa de' Medici's body.

Following some adequate time with their deceased loved one, the nurse brings Zia Erna and Tony into the ICU room to escort the Leonetti family to Zia's house. Tony's aunt offers her home to the Leonetti's family for as long as it is needed. As the hotel van arrives, the group leaves for II Bel Fior Hotel and Zia's house. Tony goes to his vehicle and returns to Zia's apartment house.

The carabinieri with Inspector Portari respectfully escort la Signora de' Medici's body to the police morgue. Upon completing his paperwork, Portari instructs his men, and then he leaves for II Bel Fior Hotel.

CHAPTER SIXTEEN

After the Leonetti family arrives at Zia's home, she encourages them to make themselves comfortable. Zia prepares a table of soups and filled panini for her guests. Completing their meal, they finish with a strong calmative tea. Zia Erna escorts them to their rooms for some rest. The Professore's son and daughter advise their father that they are leaving for Firenze to attend to their young children. But they promise to return to assist their father with any arrangements that are needed to be done. Tony says his good-byes and goes to the hotel to assist the Inspector with his continuing interrogation of the staff and other guests.

Inspector Portari arrives at II Bel Fior Hotel. He goes over to Marco's office. Standing there, in his full uniform, he seriously declares,

"I want you to assemble all your guests and staff for an important meeting."

Immediately, Marco summons his staff. He instructs them to tell the hotel guests that were present the night of Signora de' Medici's assault to assemble in the small dining room.

Portari stands erectly in front of the group and questions Marco.

"Are all the guests present who were here on the night of Signora de' Medici's assault and robbery?" Marco steps forward. He nods affirmatively to the Inspector.

Portari continues, "I've come to inform you that Signora de' Medici has died." There are gasps among the group. Some stand cold and rigid, while others wipe the tears from their eyes.

"With her death, this is now considered a felony murder case," Portari discloses. "Now I will inform each of you, of the status of your involvement to this case."

The Inspector prepares to evaluate all the vacationers at II Bel Fior Hotel. He advises them that all Italians can return to work, the children must return to school and all guests from other countries must be cleared prior to leaving.

Continuing, he states that if any guest wishes to remain they can do so. The manager of the hotel steps forward and exclaims that they will not be charged for their extended stay. The Inspector looks at the manager and proceeds with his information.

"All of you must leave all your information regarding your status and residence. I must be able to contact you immediately. The entire staff working the day of the murder must remain at their position."

"Understand?" strongly spoken by Inspector Portari.

The guests begin hurrying to Marco's office. All the arrangements are made for the leaving guests. Since there are no foreigners except Tony, the Inspector has no problem to investigate. Only six vacationers request to remain – the Montagni, Gabriella and her aunt, and the last couple, an antique dealer from Milan, the Rossini, who arrived the day after the murder.

Marco, the manager, informs the remaining guests that they will dine together for all their meals. Also, he advises them that they will retain their same rooms. Swiftly, they all retreat to their rooms.

Inspector Portari calls to Tony. As he gets close to the Inspector, Portari informs Tony that Signora de' Medici's autopsy will be done tomorrow. With heavy eyes, Tony utters softly that he's taking a break tomorrow. He's planning on hiking up the Paganella Mountain.

"This situation has revived too many old memories for me. I'll see you tomorrow evening."

The Inspector sympathizes with Tony. He agrees.

"Si, I'll see you tomorrow." Portari leaves and goes to his car.

That evening the guests take their dinner together. Tony descends to the dining room. He prepares to go into the playroom to eat alone when Gabriella steps to his side.

"Why don't you join us for dinner I promise no questions about the murder case?"

Hesitantly, Tony accepts. Upon completion of their dinner, Gabriella overhears Marco asking Tony regarding what time he is leaving for the Paganella Mountain in the morning. When the vacationers retire to their rooms, Gabriella approaches Tony.

She requests,"Tony, please I would appreciate joining you on your hike up the Paganella Mountain."

Tony looks perturbed. After a little thought, he says, "I won't be good company."

Gabriella responds, "I'll be a quiet companion."

"It's up to you. I'm leaving promptly at 7:00 am."

CHAPTER SEVENTEEN

The alarm clock shrills, making Tony jump out of bed. It's 6:30 am. He washes and dresses into his blue plaid flannel shirt and his dark brown leather hiking pants, (his lederhosen pants that Zia Erna bought for him two years ago.) Searching for his hiking boots, he finds them by the lamp table. Quickly he pulls them over his white knee high socks. Looking down to the floor he picks up his backpack and descends down the back stairs to the hotel's kitchen. There he finds Angelica preparing some panini of prosciutto, salami and cheeses. While she's placing bottles of water on the table, Tony enters.

"Bon di!" (A Tyrolean greeting), he exclaims. His cousin, Angelica chuckles as she notices Tony is looking like a Tyrolean yodeler in his hiking clothes.

Angelica continues to position a bottle of Merlot and two glasses into his backpack. Tony finishes by placing all the food into his bag.

"Grazie, this is great!" Tony exclaims, as Angelica nods with a good-natured smile.

He immediately goes to the dining room for some

espresso coffee and a sweet roll. Sitting at a table, he looks around impatiently. He mutters under his breath,

"Where the hell is she? If she doesn't come in five minutes, I'm leaving."

After a few minutes, Gabriella dressed in blue dungarees, tan suede jacket and sturdy hiking boots, dashes swiftly to Tony's table.

"I'm ready," she announces cheerfully.

Stoically, Tony tells Gabriella to sit down and have some breakfast. After a ten minute wait, Tony gets up and goes to the corner of the hallway to pick out two walking sticks. Giving Gabriella her walking stick, they position their backpacks and their sun caps. Then they say their good byes to Angelica.

Quietly they begin their walk on the road to the Paganella Mountain path. They ascend to the path mapped out by the county to start their climb up the beautiful mountain. They continue their climb without saying a word. Gabriella is occasionally out of breath, so she stops to adjust her backpack. She continues following Tony passively for about two and a half hours until they reach the Malga. This is a flattened area where the farmers and shepherds bring their flock to graze.

In the middle of this land stands an old weather beaten puckered wooden table with long wooden benches on each side of the table. Here Tony takes Gabriella's backpack and his own; he places them on the table. Gabriella sighs privately and sits down gratefully.

Tony tells Gabriella that it's lunch time. He lays out the tablecloth and places the sandwiches and drinks on the table. Gabriella empties her bag and places some apples, pears and cheese on a plate along with a small knife. Tony pours two glasses of Merlot wine and they proceed to sit down to eat.

"Buon appetito!" Tony exclaims. As they begin to eat, Tony hesitantly says, "Sorry that I was such a jerk with you. I'm having a hard time after seeing La Signora die in the hospital. Some years ago, I lost my fiancée who suffered and died from leukemia; the hospital scene is still difficult for me."

Gabriella places her hand on to Tony's hand for a second; her eyes show a large understanding. They later sit awhile admiring and sighing over the sight of the magnificent beauty of the Alps Mountains.

After cleaning up the area, they return the rest of the food into their packs. They then proceed to complete their climb to the top of the Paganella Mountain. Walking for another hour, they reach the top of the mountain.

Gabriella and Tony stand immobile as they are enraptured at the site of the white majestic cathedral snow peaks on the top of these gigantic mountains. Each of them could feel the touch and the crowning of the sunshine embracing and encircling them.

Tears rolled down Gabriella's eyes. She looks at Tony, without realizing it, they both warmly embrace. Tony softly kisses Gabriella on the lips. They stand still as one.

Realizing what happened, Tony quickly pulls away and apologies.

"It's okay." Gabriella gently smiles.

Each takes their own backpack and walk to the comfort station before they start their descent. Calmly, they climb down the mountain. It takes a shorter time of three hours. When they reach the bottom, they walk silently to the hotel.

Gabriella looks kindly at Tony.

"Grazie for a wonderful experience."

Tony agrees, but something makes him feel uncomfortable. His detective instinct kicks in, impelling him to be careful with Gabriella.

CHAPTER EIGHTEEN

Tony goes quickly to his room. He checks his messages on his cell phone. One of the messages is from Portari asking him to come to his office in Trento this evening.

Swiftly, he showers and dresses into sport clothes. Immediately he returns the Inspector's call.

"Pronto, Antonio, it's Tony."

The Inspector quickly answers the telephone and advises Tony,

"Please come to my office this evening. I want to show you the autopsy report."

Tony replies. "Okay, I'll be there about 8 o'clock."

"Ciao. See you in my office," the Inspector responds.

Tony sits down to eat his dinner with the six remaining guests at the hotel. He remains casual and pleasant. No one speaks except Signora Montagni. She inquires about Professore Leonetti. Tony answers that he's doing the best that can be expected, under the circumstances. After finishing his espresso, Tony excuses himself. Briskly he enters his car for his trip to Trento.

Reaching the carabinieri's post, he enters and sees Portari sitting at the front desk.

"Ciao, Antonio ." The Inspector looks up and requests that Tony take a seat. He hands him a cup of coffee. Tony declines.

"Here's the autopsy report." Tony takes it carefully into his hands.

CHAPTER NINETEEN

AUTOPSY REPORT OF SIGNORA LOUISA de' MEDICI

The wound at the back of head – a deep 10 cm. laceration at the site of Medulla Oblongata caused the clotting at the base of the brain.

The formation of the embolism at the base of the brain caused the patient, Louisa de' Medici, to go into respiratory failure and cardiac arrest.

The origin of the embolism was found located at the base of the brain.

Probability: The bleeding and clotting occurred from the trauma of a heavy object.

The forensic collection at the site of the crime:

The blood stain on the marble statue of Julius Caesar bust (weighing 4.5 kg) was examined and tested. The laboratory confirmed that the blood stain on the statue is RH type AB positive. It proved to be the same blood type as Louisa de' Medici's, the victim. No finger prints were found on the statue.

Tony looks up, "Guess we're searching for a murderer now."

Inspector listens, and then responds, "I'm investigating with other polizia agencies, especially the ones from Firenze, in search of the black market for old art masterpieces. They have a greater pool of knowledge of the Art world than I have."

"Tomorrow I will go to your aunt's house to see Professore Leonetti regarding the autopsy report and the release of La Signora's body for her funeral. We will assist him in all the needed transportation."

Tony leaves the station house and goes to his car; he sees lights in the basement of the museum across the street. He doesn't remember any lights being on in the museum basement prior to his visit with Portari. His mind swirls, he knows it's after hours; he gets a gut feeling, his detective premonition, so he decides swiftly and quietly to walk down the stairs to the basement windows. He squeezes his body into the corner of the basement window panes. He sees two women standing with a tall slim man. He can't make out the persons. Suddenly the lights are turned off. Tony waits; he's startled, as he recognizes one of the cars.

His heart leaps "It's Gabriella's car!"

Baffled, Tony's mind turns, "What is she doing here, in the museum at these late hours?"

"Who's the man in the museum? Could it be Dottore Franzoi, or is it Roberto?"

All he knows is that he must be cautious with Gabriella, not letting her know what he has seen. Carefully, he takes out his cell phone and calls Portari, informing him of all that has transpired at the museum this evening.

Inspector responds, "Keep a record of all that's happened.

We will pool all our facts together. Now I must get ready for La Signora's funeral. See you tomorrow at the hotel."

His mind is in turmoil. Tony quickly returns to his hotel.

CHAPTER TWENTY

Next morning, the Inspector Portari arrives at Zia Erna's house. He knocks at the door. Zia Erna cordially invites him into the kitchen. Responsively, the Professore gets up from his chair and urges him to sit down. Zia presses the Inspector to have some coffee. He declines politely. Zia excuses herself and ambles out into her backyard garden.

Portari sits by Professore Leonetti's side as he begins to inform him about the autopsy report.

He speaks gently, "Si, it has been confirmed that the cause of La Signora de' Medici's death, as documented by the medical examiner," The Inspector stops and looks at the Professore. Then he continues,

"The injury to La Signora's head caused her cardiac arrest. The trauma and the attack on Signora de' Medici is now considered a murder case." The Professore lowers his head into a soft sigh.

While raising his head, he asks in a low voice, "What happens now?"

The Inspector tells him that the first priority is a proper funeral for his wife. Professore's gaze is locked on the Inspector. He waits for some advice. Ispettore Portari suggests that the Professore telephone his adult children. He will tell them what steps need to be taken.

The Professore takes out his telefonino and dials his son's number.

He answers, "Pronto, Luigi. Si, it's Papa. I want you and your sister to speak to Ispettore Portari to arrange your mother's funeral." He pauses.

"Si. It's been confirmed by the autopsy report" (his voice trembling) "That your mother was murdered. Please, both of you make proper arrangements in Firenze at the Cathedral of Santa Maria Magdalena for Mama's funeral Mass.

"Ciao. I will pass you over to speak to Ispettore Portari." The telefonino is handed to the Inspector.

Portari cordially says, "I will be at your service at all times. You make all the arrangements. Call me and we shall arrange an escorted transportation to the funeral home in Firenze."

"Grazie!" responds Luigi." I'll start the process immediately."

The Inspector expresses his condolences to the Leonetti family and departs.

The Professore continues talking with his son regarding some personal requests.

The Professore's offspring tell their father that they will return to Trento to accompany him with the return of their mother's body to Firenze for her respectful funeral.

Now it's only time to wait for the completed arrangements.

CHAPTER TWENTY-ONE

In the middle of the week, Luigi and Anita Leonetti call their father with the arrangements for their mother's funeral.

"Ciao Papa. Come va?" There's a long silence. Luigi hesitates, and then he begins telling his father that all the arrangements for the funeral Mass are completed.

His father interrupts, "Did you speak with Ispettore Portari?"

"Si. We confirmed all the particulars with him."

"Papa, the funeral Mass will be said next Friday at the Cathedral of Santa Maria Magdalena in Firenze. We will arrive at the hotel early on Wednesday morning to go with you to Firenze. The Ispettore advised us that he and his men will escort us, with Mama's body, via train transportation to the funeral parlor in Firenze."

Quietly the Professore's son respectfully reviews the preparations for the next week.

Luigi continues in a soft tone,

"Papa, the arrangements are made for the following week: Wednesday, we will depart by train at 10:00 am from Trento to Firenze with Mama's body."

Hesitantly, he waits for his father's response. Hearing nothing, he resumes.

"On Thursday, since the de' Medici family are well known benefactors of Firenze, Cardinal Bernadine of Milan asked for Mama's wake to be available for public viewing at the Santa Maria Magdalena Cathedral from 11:00 am to 4:00pm."

"The following day, Friday, the funeral Mass will begin at 11:00 am, officiated by Cardinal Bernadine of Milan. Since Mama was a dedicated volunteer and contributor to the education for the homeless and the poor children, he requested the honor to celebrate her Mass. Also, many of the nuns and the clergy from Firenze will be present at the Mass." Their father is listening quietly.

Luigi hands the telefonino to his sister Anita.

She tells her father,

"Sister Martha informed us that a choir of children will be singing at the funeral Mass."

Their father sighs, "Bene! Your mother will be pleased." (As he looked up to the heavens)

The Professore asks of his son, "I need for you to reserve a couple of rows in church for the hotel's Trentini who wish to attend the funeral Mass."

"It will be done," Luigi affirms.

"Well done, figli!" Professore Leonetti lovingly responds to his daughter and son. Finishing his conversation he says, "See you next Wednesday morning."

The Professore telephones Tony to come over to his aunt's house. As Tony arrives, the Professore ask Zia Erna and Tony to sit down. He proceeds to retell to them all the arrangements of the funeral.

Tony requests respectfully "Could we attend the funeral Mass? It would be our honor."

With moistened eyes the Professore looks up. "We will

be pleased to have you, your family members and any hotel guests who wish to attend."

Tony nods, "I'll advise Marco of the plans for Signora de' Medici's funeral Mass."

Tony leaves. He goes to the hotel's office to speak with Marco regarding La Signora de' Medici's Mass. Marco listens and takes notes carefully.

"I will make all the arrangements for all the persons at the hotel who want to attend La Signora's funeral Mass."

Tony hurries down the corridor to his room. He quickly calls the Inspector on his cell phone.

"Pronto, Antonio, we heard about the plans for La Signora de' Medici funeral. Zia and I will most certainly be attending."

The Inspector retorts, "I'm glad you called. I received strong information regarding the possibility of recovering the stolen da Vinci masterpiece. When I go to Firenze with La Signora de' Medici's body next Wednesday, I will visit with the Inspector General of the Polizia in Firenze to procure more information."

Tony exclaims excitedly and boldly, "Bravo! maybe we will be closer to capturing the murderer. Ciao. See you soon."

CHAPTER TWENTY-TWO

Later Marco posts the arrangements for Signora Louisa de' Medici's funeral Mass on the bulletin board. He proceeds to the dining room to explain the notice to the guests. He advises them that he can only take ten people in the hotel van. They must see him to obtain a seat for Friday morning's trip to Firenze.

After clearing away all the dining room dishes, Mirella scurries to Marco's office. She tells him that her mother, Bruna D'Amici and she will attend the funeral Mass.

Marco looks up. His brow wrinkles with confusion. Mirella hesitantly but quickly adds that her mother was a childhood friend of La Signora de' Medici when she vacationed in the Trentino region as a child.

"Alright! I'll put you both on the list for Friday morning."

After much murmuring and whispering among the guests, the ones who wish to attend the funeral Mass make their arrangements with Marco.

Coming out of the kitchen, Mario, the chef goes to Marco's office. He advises Marco that the other two brothers and he will remain back at the hotel. They will not go to the funeral Mass. They will stay at the hotel and prepare the food for the returning guests.

Marco replies, "That's fine!" He stops and looks at Mario with concern, "Is everything okay?"

"Sure, of course," as he swiftly returns to speak with his brothers in the hotel's kitchen.

That evening the completed list is posted on the bulletin board:

LA SIGNORA LOUISA de' MEDICI's
FUNERAL MASS

Next week, Friday 11:00 am at the Cathedral of Santa Maria Magdalena, Firenze

ATTENDEES: Mirella and Bruna D'Amici
Erna Zini and Tony Pacelli
Angelica and Marco Zini
Maria and Paolo Montagni
Gabriella Longhi and Sylvia Bonetti

Please meet in front of II Bel Fior Hotel promptly at 5:00 am. We will not wait for lateness. We will return that evening, at approximately 6:30 pm.

Dinner will be served at 7:30 pm that evening. Grazie.

Marco Zini
Manager

CHAPTER TWENTY-THREE

The following Wednesday, a limousine drops the Professore's offspring, Anita and Luigi, at the II Bel Fior Hotel. They arrive around half past eight in the morning. They take their hand bags and rush across the street to Zia Erna's apartment where they find their father, who is slowly eating his breakfast. As they fondly embrace their father, Zia quickly scurries to their side, asking them, if they need to refresh themselves. While they make themselves comfortable, they sit near their father and begin eat some breakfast. Zia brings out the carafe of coffee and warm milk and leaves it on the table.

"Si accomodi. Please take some coffee, sweet rolls, yogurts and some fresh fruits," Zia generously offers.

Feeling revived, the Leonetti family goes to the hotel, waiting for Marco the manager to take them to Trento.

At the morgue, the Mayor of Trento, Signor Bruno Polli, is attentively waiting for the Leonetti family to give his respectful condolences prior to the police's accompaniment of La Signora de' Medici's body to Firenze.

The body of La Signora is prepared by the mortician for the trip to Firenze. Marco takes the Leonetti family to the morgue in Trento to view their deceased loved one, prior to boarding the train for their trip to Firenze.

After the Leonetti family accepts the condolences from the Mayor, Inspector Portari and his carabinieri, correctly dressed in full uniform, escort the body to the train. The Inspector explains that it will take approximately a little more than four hours to arrive in Firenze. The Inspector considerately attends to the comforts of this bereaved family.

As the train approaches the train station in Firenze, Portari looks out of the window and notices an escort of policemen lined at the train station ready to receive the casket and the family. The police lieutenant and the funeral director climb the train stairs to consult with the Leonetti family. Following a short discussion, the family descends from the train. The casket goes to the funeral parlor while the policemen escort the family to their home in Fiesole.

Inspector Portari says his goodbyes and notifies the family that he has assigned a couple of carabinieri to remain with La Signora's body until the burial.

The Professore bows his head, looks up at the Inspector, "Grazie." He answers with appreciation.

The Inspector instructs his men. Swiftly he walks across the main street into the Piazza. Looking around he locates the tall red brick building with a large sign, POLIZIA, on the side of the building. He enters the building for his appointment with Ispettore Generale Odericci.

CHAPTER TWENTY-FOUR

The Inspector enters into the front room and sees a young sergeant sitting at the front desk, he says,

"I'm Ispettore Antonio Portari from Trento. I have an appointment to see Ispettore Generale Odericci."

The sergeant picks up the phone and dials the Inspector General's office. He speaks sotto voce that an Inspector Portari from Trento is in the office to see him. Inspector Odericci responds that he will be right out. The officer politely advises Portari to have a seat. A few minutes later, Inspector Odericci, a tall thin middle aged man with slightly balding coppery red hair and searching brown eyes approaches Inspector Portari.

"You're Ispettore Portari?"

"Si."

The Inspector General extends his hand amicably. "Piacere. Please come to my office."

As Antonio sits down, the Inspector Generale hands him a cup of coffee. "Help yourself," pointing to a couple of sandwiches that are sitting in a tray on his desk.

"Make yourself comfortable. I know you've had a long trip."

"No, I'm fine. I had a panino on the train. Grazie!" Portari is in a hurry to eagerly acquire all the information that Inspector Odericci possesses.

Inspector Odericci continues,

"First, I want to inform you that some of my officers and I have been working on this case since Signora Louisa de' Medici announced that she was loaning her da Vinci masterpiece to the Trentino museum."

"We're so sorry for the murder of La Signora de' Medici. We only wish to help you with the solving of her murder and the recuperation of the treasured masterpiece."

Inspector Odericci continues with his information.

"We have knowledge through underground informants that the masterpiece is still in Trento, and it will be up for sale at the Trentino museum this coming Monday."

Inspector Portari quickly straightens his back and sits on the edge of his seat with sharpened eyes,

"Who gave you this information?"

Inspector Odericci says, "I cannot disclose these facts at present, but I will give you all the information in a couple of days. I don't want to jeopardize our undercover plan."

Inspector Odericci resumes, "This weekend I will keep you abreast of our larger plan. Hopefully you will have your case solved too. It will be our great pleasure to assist you in putting an end to this tragedy."

"By the way, as per your request, we arranged for your rental car. It's available in our police garage. Our sergeant will assist you in locating your rental car."

Inspector Portari extends his hand and thanks him, and then he leaves to go to the police garage. His mind is enthusiastically swirling with all this information.

Quickly he rushes to his rental car for his return trip to Trento.

CHAPTER TWENTY-FIVE

Antonio Portari reaches his condo apartment in Trento late Wednesday evening. He picks up his telefonino and calls Tony.

"Ciao, Tony. I just returned from Firenze where I spoke with Ispettore Odericci. He informs me that his police department has been following the da Vinci masterpiece since La Signora de' Medici announced that she was loaning her da Vinci painting to the Trentino museum. Through underground informants, Odericci knows that the masterpiece is still in Trento. There's strong intelligence that the stolen da Vinci masterpiece will be up for sale this coming Monday."

Tony listens intensely and anxiously. He inquires, "Who are these informants?"

Portari continues, "He cannot disclose this information at present because it could jeopardize his plans. Inspector Odericci told me he will keep us abreast of their larger plan. We will then work together to capture the murderer or murderers."

"Well done!" Tony exclaims excitedly.

"Tomorrow, I'm going to the medical examiner's office

to review all the evidence. Then I'm coming to the hotel," Portari discloses.

"Okay. I'll prepare Marco and Zia for our revaluation of the crime room and the people at the hotel," Tony retorts.

Putting down his cell phone, Tony goes to the hallway and looks down the stairs. He sees Marco's office lights on. Descending down the stairs, he goes to the first floor. Tony enters Marco's office, sits down and tells Marco that Inspector Portari needs to re-examine the crime room for another review of all the evidence.

Tony informs Marco, "He may need to interrogate the staff and the guests again."

Marco stiffly replies, "I'm tired of all these interferences. The hotel business is suffering. It has to come to a conclusion."

"Stay strong, Marco. We are working hard. I think we're getting close." Tony reacts.

"Ciao, Marco. See you in the morning."

CHAPTER TWENTY-SIX

The following morning, the Inspector goes to the medical examiner's office to pick up the reports on all the forensic evidence collected. He reassesses that the only fingerprints that they uncovered were those of Mirella and Mirro from the doorknob of the crime room. Both had an alibi, as they were the ones who prepared the Signora de' Medici's room. The Inspector assumes that the murderer must have worn gloves.

Before Portari puts the papers back into the envelope, he takes another look at the end of the autopsy report. Once more he reads that the blood stain on the base of the Julius Caesar's marble statue was RH AB positive, the same as Louisa de' Medici, the victim's blood type. No fingerprints were found on the statue. He ponders a moment, and then he replaces all the documents back into its proper folder.

The Inspector heads his car to II Bel Fior Hotel. As he arrives, Tony is crossing the street to have breakfast with his aunt. Tony looks over and waves to the Inspector. He rushes back to the hotel.

Grabbing two cups of coffee, they go to the back office of the hotel to talk. After a brief discussion, they go to

Marco's office to retrieve the crime room's key. Marco looks annoyed and unusually agitated as he follows them to the crime room. He opens the door and sternly demands,

"Take your time but stay out of my way and make sure you return the key only to me." He dashes away.

Inspector Portari takes out some ink pads then opens some formaldehyde lab bottles. He places them on special paper on top of the desk.

Putting on latex gloves, he begins his search of the room. He's completely engrossed in his work that he ignores Tony in the room.

Tony just sits watches and waits for instructions. Using a fluorescent lamp, the Inspector dusts for prints on the window sill, on the chairs and even on the wooden floor.

Tony thinks to himself, "This has been done before by forensics."

Any kind of pins or items on the carpet Inspector Portari picks up with his tweezers. He's obsessed with the hope of finding something that was missed immediately after the crime.

Tony realizes that the Inspector has to leave no clue unturned. He is determined to solve this murder.

When the Inspector is satisfied, he steps out of the room in search of some hotel workers. He almost forgets that Tony is still in the room. Looking back at Tony, without an explanation, he requests

"Tony, please return the key."

Tony goes to Marco's office. Since Marco doesn't look up from his paperwork, Tony just puts the key on the desk, turns around and leaves.

With a determined decisiveness, Portari goes looking for Mirella and Mirro in the dining room.

Approaching these workers the Inspector seriously asks,

"Please tell me again what you were doing when Signora de' Medici arrived at the hotel the night of the assault?"

Mirro smugly responds, "I got Mirella to open the door of Signora de' Medici's room. Then my men and I unloaded the luggage of La Signora into her room. That's all. Then I re-locked the room's door. How many more times must I repeat this?" he answers loudly.

"Okay." Inspector Portari tells them to go back to work.

Then Portari shouts after them, "But stay available."

Tony and the Inspector return to the back office. There Portari advises Tony that he must return the rest of his collection to forensics.

"Ciao, Tony. See you at the funeral Mass."

The Inspector hurries to his car. The car screeches. Tony realizes that this case is fraying on all their nerves. He goes to check on his aunt.

Tomorrow the funeral will be another hard day for all of them, again.

CHAPTER TWENTY-SEVEN

- The day of the funeral –

The morning is wet and foggy after a night of rain. It's 4:45 am. Marco is outside the hotel preparing the hotel van for the trip to Firenze. He places all the water and sandwiches into the back cooler of the bus. Then he puts a large thermos of coffee next to the cooler.

A small black Peugeot car arrives. Out come, Mirella and her mother.

Mirella introduces her mother to Marco.

"This is my mother, Bruna D'Amici."

Marco observes a sixty year old, tall, well-formed woman who dresses in a stylish manner. She has silver blonde hair and light blue eyes. Her oval face is perfectly made-up. She nods with a faint smile. Both mother and daughter wear stylish tan iridescent raincoats with matching hats and umbrellas. Quickly they enter the van to sit in the back.

The next to exit from the hotel are the Montagni , then Gabriella and her aunt. The last to arrive is Zia Erna and Angelica. As they enter they say, "Buon giorno" to all the passengers.

Zia Erna advises the group that there are some refreshments available for their trip.

Marco gives his instructions. He tells his passengers that the trip will take approximately five hours, and he will make a toilette break in about two hours.

Before taking off, Tony arrives and says a quick, "Buon giorno".

He sits in the bucket seat next to Marco to assist him with the navigation.

Off they go to the autostrada. The ride is a quiet one since everyone is still sleepy.

After a rest stop, each passenger takes some refreshment. The passengers indulge in either a fruit yogurt or a panino of jam and butter.

Then Marco proceeds to Firenze.

Arriving at the Cathedral of Santa Maria Magdalena, they all pile out of the van. It's 10:15 am.

Marco directs his group. "Go to the ushers where they will escort you to your reserved pew, and they will attend to any of your needs."

He continues, "Tony and I will place the van in the allocated area for buses outside of the main areas. We will see you in a little while."

As the hotel group enters the cathedral, they are greeted by soft Bach music. They sit attentively in their reserved seats, observing the magnificent arrangement of flowers and the activities surrounding them.

After parking the hotel van in the public square, Marco and Tony return to the cathedral and sit behind their hotel group. Tony looks around the church until he finds Inspector Portari. They nod to each other.

CHAPTER TWENTY-EIGHT

They all sit and wait for the service to begin.

The cathedral is filled with the Florentine community who loved and worked with La Signora de' Medici. There are contingents of dignitaries from Firenze and Trento. Mayor Pasi, Bishop Montavi, and Dottore Franzoi of the Trentino museum are sitting in the front rows with the Leonetti family. The relatives of La Signora are seated next to the Leonetti family.

Ispettore Generale Odericci and Ispettore Portari are sitting a few rows behind the Leonetti friends.

A choir of children sits at the side of the altar. Sister Martha, a close friend of La Signora, is directing them with their hymns.

The children are dressed in their white shirts, navy blue skirts for the girls and navy blue trousers for the boys; the organ plays and the children are ready to sing their hearts out.

As the music plays the children sing "Come to God's table."

The body of Louisa de' Medici is rolled reverently and slowly down the aisle. The Leonetti family follows in unison each carrying a long stemmed white rose. The grandchildren are dressed in white, celebrating the life of Louisa de' Medici, their beloved grandmother. The Mass proceeds to the communion, where the children sing "Panis Angelicus" (The Bread of Angels.)

At the homily, Cardinal Bernadine of Milan speaks.

"I can still see La Signora de' Medici's smiling face as she helped the children in the schools and hospitals with their arts and crafts projects. Thank you God for her generous life." The children finish their hymns by singing the "Ave Maria."

At the end of the Mass, Luigi, Louisa's son renders his mother's eulogy. His eyes are moist with tears.

"I remember, La Mama sitting at the kitchen table, her favorite place. She enjoyed arranging the paintings and drawings with her grandchildren." (He needs to stop for a moment, and then he continues.) "My mother studied the Arts at the University of Firenze. She gave back to the children and the community her knowledge and skills in the Arts and Sculpture."

"I overheard people calling my mother, "The Lady of Smiles." He concludes, "When you think of her, think only of the good things in her life, please." He pauses, his voice is cracking. "Remember La Mama**'s smiling face."**

Tony is sitting in the back of the church. Quietly he grabs an occasional look around the cathedral, searching for reactions during the ceremonies. He doesn't observe much, but he does notice Mirella has her head bent low and Gabriella is combing the church instead of focusing on the Mass. Tony's greatly annoyed and he thinks, "What's that all about."

At the conclusion of the service, Luigi stands up by the altar rail and relates,

"When my parents went to New York City after the 9/11

Twin Towers tragedy, they heard "Amazing Grace" sang at St. Patrick's Cathedral in New York City; My mother was so moved by this hymn, that we want to lead her to God with this hymn."

They all leave the cathedral with triumphal sounds of "Amazing Grace."

CHAPTER TWENTY-NINE

The Leonetti family presses onward for La Signora's private burial in the cemetery of Fiesole, their home town. The ushers advise the hotel group that there are refreshments and accommodations, prior to their return trip, in the basement of the cathedral. The ushers lead their distant guests to the catered food and the toilettes. Tony and Marco urge the hotel group to go to the basement and refresh themselves before they begin their long trip back home.

"We'll return in thirty minutes to take you back to II Bel Fior Hotel."

Returning to the outside square of Firenze, Tony and Marco take care of their needs and check on the hotel van. They finally sit in the bus and enjoy some panini with salami and broccoli rabe. After a cup of coffee, they feel refreshed.

They then proceed to Santa Maria Magdalena Cathedral to collect their passengers for their return trip to the hotel.

Everyone climbs into the van, returning to their same seat. On the trip back, the passengers agree that the service was not only memorable but that they experienced the thrill of God's love. Marco does another rest stop, after a two hour drive. He offers his passengers some water or coffee before they resume their drive home. Finally, they arrive at the hotel at 6:35 pm.

Zia Erna announces to the guests that supper will be served at the hotel at 7:30pm.

Mirella escorts her mother to her car. Tony quickly follows them.

"I'm glad you came. I understand that you were a childhood friend of La Signora," looking at Mirella's mother.

Bruna D'Amici answers, "Si. We played as children." Bruna D'Amici replies, as she stares at her daughter Mirella. She continues hurriedly. "I must get back to the Hotel Americana. I'm working this evening."

Mirella doesn't look at Tony. She exclaims, "I must go into the hotel to help out with dinner."

Tony's cell phone goes off. He answers,

"Pronto, ciao, Antonio. We have just arrived at II Bel Fior Hotel."

The Inspector responds, "It's been a long day. I'll see you tomorrow at noon. I have much to tell you."

"Okay. See you tomorrow," Tony replies.

Tony's tired so he goes to the kitchen to get a tray of food. Putting his tray on the foyer table he enters the dining room to say his good night to all the guests. He leans over and kisses his aunt.

Quickly, he rushes to his room to enjoy a quiet meal. Tony needs to review and evaluate all his notes. He has to include all that he has observed today and in the past weeks. He must be ready for tomorrow's conference with Inspector Portari.

Tony showers and goes to his bed. His night sleep

becomes uneasy. He's constantly tossing and turning around in bed. His mind is searching incessantly for facts and conclusions. He finally dozes off to sleep in the early morning hours.

CHAPTER THIRTY

Late Saturday morning Tony rises, dresses quickly and goes down to the hotel kitchen to pick up a caffè latte and a freshly baked roll. Finishing his breakfast, he searches on the side table for his folder of notes on the de' Medici case. Tony picks them up and takes off with tenacious determination to see the Inspector in Trento. He parks his car behind the carabinieri's station. Entering the carabinieri's post, Tony sees Inspector Portari sitting at the front desk,

"Come to my office. I have much to tell you." Portari urges Tony, to quickly follow him.

After they get seated in the Inspector's office, Portari divulges:

"I received a message from Inspector Odericci. His PLAN is in progress. With the help of Professore Martini, the manager of the Uffizi Galleria, Inspector Odericci will arrange with Dottore Franzoi, the director of the Museo di Buon Consiglio, for their deliveries of the two crates of artifacts, for his annual Trentino Christmas Show.

"In Firenze, Professore Martini and Inspector Odericci will replace each crate of supposed artifacts with one police officer. Dottore Franzoi will NOT be in on their plan.

These two expected crates, with police escort, will arrive this Monday afternoon at the Museo di Buon Consiglio. This loan of antiques is usually done every year with this Trentino museum, so no one will suspect anything different."

Tony listens closely, "What's the purpose of the officers inside the crates?"

"This coming Monday, we have strong information that the masterpiece, da Vinci's smaller "Annunciation" will be up for under-cover sale at this Trentino museum. We need the police officers inside the museum to unlock the Arts basement metal door to allow us to enter and arrest the alleged criminals."

Portari looks at Tony, "Your face looks puzzled."

Tony inquires, "How will the crates be cared for?"

"The crates will be transported and driven by two Florentine police officers in a canvas covered truck. The other two policemen who are designated for the aerated crates will remain outside of the crates while traveling to Trento. Their comforts of food and toilette will be attended to prior to reaching the Trentino museum. The officers will have full control of opening and closing the simple locks inside of their designated crate. Once they arrive at the Trentino museum, the police contained crates will be moved and placed in the corner of the basement's Arts room. In this area there are facilities for toilette and drinks."

Tony's relieved. "You certainly have fine tuned this whole plan." He continues with one more inquiry. "Who is this informant who is helping you?"

"We will be advised appropriately at the right time. Inspector Odericci doesn't want to jeopardize their larger plan."

"Okay, I'm in. I want this mystery to end. There are too many lies amidst."

"Tony, have courage. All will be resolved. II Bel Fior Hotel will be restored to its prior reputation."

Before leaving, Tony turns to the Inspector and leaves his de' Medici's case notes. "I'll give you my completed notes on Monday.

By the way, I'm going to see my father's relatives in Tenno near Riva del Garda tomorrow."

Portari smiles at Tony. "That's fine. I think you need a break. Ciao."

CHAPTER THIRTY-ONE

The Sunday bells are chiming from the church belfry. Tony counts the chimes, nine! His mind notes "It's 9am."

He dresses and is ready to go to Mass at Saint Raphael's church which is only three minutes from the hotel. He hurries over and enters the side door of the church. Fortunately, he finds a seat at the back of the church. The church is filled with the town's people and the tourists who are getting ready to leave at the end of their vacations.

The Mass just started. Tony looks around and sees Zia Erna and Angelica in the middle pew. He smiles and winks at them. Then his gaze spots Gabriella and her aunt who are sitting on the left side of the church. Gabriella catches his eyes. Tony nods stiffly. Lately he finds it hard to smile at her.

After the Mass is over, Tony walks down the road and enters a tobacco shop to purchase an American newspaper. With the newspaper in hand, he strolls into a café across the street to have an espresso and a sweet roll. He spends a half hour peacefully reading his newspaper.

Refreshed, he rushes to his vehicle. On the seat of his

car, he finds a large apple strudel cake. He smiles with a little laugh, as he knows that it must have been Zia who placed it in his car, for him to bring it to his relatives in Tenno, near Riva del Garda.

The trip will take around an hour, taking the side roads without traveling on the autostrada.

CHAPTER THIRTY-TWO

Tony arrives at his cousin Alcede's vineyards around noontime. He catches sight of the uniformed rows of grapevine basking in the brilliant sunshine. The vines are filled with plump, bursting golden yellow grapes.

Tony reflects proudly, (This region makes the best Chardonnay wine in Italy.)

Seeing his cousin Alcede in the fields, Tony rushes over and gives Alcede a quick slap on his back, then they fondly bear-hug embrace.

Looking up at Tony, smilingly his cousin announces, "It's about time you came to visit."

"Well, you know all about the problems Zia has been having, the thefts, and the murder."

With immense concern, Alcede answers, "I'm so sorry for your aunt because she was doing such a fine job with the hotel after your Zio Beppe died."

After a moment of silence, Alcede says, "Okay, let's go down to see the ladies, as they are very anxious to see you."

They both run down the hill to the cobblestone street, under the stone arches; they walk towards Alcede's medieval stone house. The outside of his house remains in the tradition of the 16th and the 17th century Italian architecture. As per the Italian laws, the structure of this community, Tenno near Riva del Garda cannot be changed; it must be preserved for its Italian history and architecture. This is the same region where some vacationing English poets, like Robert Browning wrote some of his delightful romantic poems.

As Alcede unlocks the front door, Tony and his cousin enter into a modern household, where the first room is the living room with an ensemble of soft maroon leather sofa and chairs. The floor is laid out into delicate almond-veined ceramic tiles, which spread forward from the corridor to the kitchen.

Alcede opens the mahogany glass paneled door to an elongated kitchen. To the right side of the wall stand large silver refrigerator, a matching stove and a dishwasher. As they trot to the long pine knotted table, there stands Alcede's wife, Livia, and his daughters Gina and Roberta, preparing and cutting up the food for their sumptuous Italian banquet.

As Tony walks towards the ladies, they quickly run to hug him. They surround him like they are doing the Tarantella dance.

They all sit at the kitchen table, trying to get an update about the mystery at the hotel. Tony summarizes hurriedly but briefly.

Tony continues, "Be assured we will uncover these criminals." He says soberly.

To change the conversation, Tony asks "Any news?"

"Si, Gina's getting married next spring, we hope you can come."

"It would be my honor."

"We'll keep you to that promise."

Livia gets up and gives each person a plethora of foods to take out for their banquet in the vineyards.

Two other families of relatives arrive to join in the outdoor festivities. They total fifteen persons at the long wooden table. The meal consists of garden vegetable antipasto, homemade pasta béchamel, roasted rabbit, and a loin of pork in wine gravy, a large polenta with sauerkraut, and green beans.

Before the start of the meal, Alcede filled with pride, hands each guest a cluster of his golden grapes.

Immediately, Tony pops a grape into his mouth, it explodes into sugary juices dripping down the side of his chin.

"Wow!" Tony wipes his chin with his napkin, and lifts his glass of wine, "You're going to get first prize this year for your Chardonnay."

They all smile and grin.

After consuming their main meal, they sit back and enjoy telling humorous stories about their youth, while they continue to taste the wonderful quality of Alcede's wines.

After a refreshing afternoon, Livia lays out a large spread of sweets, which all the guests contributed to compliment the cappuccino and espresso caffè with grappa. Each person could choose from apple strudel, multi flavored gelatos, a plum cream torte, chocolate mousse and some fresh cut fruits.

More than four hours pass, the smiles and laughter make for an experience that could heal even the saddest of souls.

Close to 6pm, Tony stands up, patting his tummy, "The meal was great, mostly you all are great!

I'm sorry to leave, but I must get back to the hotel because we have much to do tomorrow."

Everyone remains quiet, as they know that Tony is involved in serious business.

Alcede gets up and hands Tony six assorted bottles of his Merlot and Chardonnay wines, Thrilled, Tony embraces everyone at the table and he promises,

"Next time, I will stay to help you with the harvest."

"We'll wait for you." They said with a knowing smile.

CHAPTER THIRTY-THREE

Tony takes off to the Bel Fior Hotel, this time via the autostrada. Arriving at the hotel, he runs up the stairs to his aunt's apartment to give her two bottles of his cousins' wines. Zia is so grateful for the gift, as she has high regard for his relative's wines. He doesn't stay, but he kisses his aunt on the cheeks and says his good night. He's eager to go to his room, as he has all his paper work to review.

Dashing into the II Bel Fior Hotel, Tony encounters Marco, the hotel manager.

Marco looks dejected. Tony's cousin exclaims, "Most of the hotel guests will be leaving tomorrow."

"Good, don't worry, you'll get back your hotel's reputation." Tony encourages.

Marco's eyes fall to the ground, "Spero, I hope so." He whispers. Tony quickly saunters to his room to examine his notes for his big day with the Inspector.

Tony can't get to sleep; he puts on his pajamas and ambles out to his room's terrace.

Looking up at the moonlit Alpine Mountains, with the autumn breezes gently easing into the night, he sighs,

"God, I hope this crisis is over soon."

Searching for some answers, his eyes wander to the driveway. Tony moves into the dark bend of the terrace, he sees Mirro pacing back and forth, smoking feverishly, and stepping on one butt after another.

"Someone's nervous!" Tony muses, thinking of the many unanswered troubling questions that he has.

After Mirro leaves, Tony enters his bedroom, organizes his notes and assessments for Inspector Portari. He makes a special point to report all that he has seen this evening in the driveway.

CHAPTER THIRTY-FOUR

Tony tries to get some sleep. His mind and body are so worked up that he gets up early in the morning. While dressing into his dark grey sweats, his mind wanders into many complicated questions. Putting aside his notes, he decides to call his Mom in NYC.

Considering the time in New York City, Tony wonders if his Mom will be asleep yet. But he needs the comfort of her voice, so he dials her number.

"Hi Mom, did I wake you?"

"No, Tony, I was just getting myself ready for bed.

It's so good to hear from you. How are you?" She asks.

Tony quickly responds, "Good! We're trying to resolve all the problems over here. Hopefully we'll get the answers this week. Mom, I'm probably coming home this Friday. I'll call again, to confirm my definite plans."

"We'll be so happy to see you. Please give my regards to my sister Erna."

"Mom we'll talk a long time when I get home."

"Tony, I pray for a satisfactory outcome."

"Thanks Mom, it's a tough road. See you soon!"

Tony puts his documents into his briefcase and goes

down to the hotel's kitchen. Mirro is sitting with an espresso in hand, his eyes are reddened with dark circles, and his head is bent low.

Tony approaches him with concern and some suspicion.

"Didn't sleep well, can I help you with anything? I'm a good listener."

(Tony wonders if something is bothering Mirro's conscience.)

Mirro dismisses his cousin and jumps off his stool. Immediately he walks away from Tony.

Tony takes a long sip of his caffè latte, picks up his jacket and briefcase, and runs to his automobile. With a suitcase filled with his completed investigative notes, he precedes to Trento to see Inspector Portari.

CHAPTER THIRTY-FIVE

Tony's mind is spinning with so many thoughts that he doesn't pay attention to his driving, until he finds that he's has already arrived in Trento. Disturbed, he sits still for a moment.

He tells himself that he must keep his mind straight, as he has many serious matters to deal with, ahead of him.

Tony places his car in the reserve area behind the carabinieri's office. As he opens the door he sees a young officer who is sitting by his desk. He recognizes Tony.

"Buon giorno!" Tony responds to the police officer.

"I'm going down to Inspector Portari's office."

The young policeman answers, "Si, he's expecting you."

As Tony strolls to the Inspector's office, he notices that the door is wide open.

"Ciao, Tony, come in. How is it going?"

In a disgruntled manner, not in his usual calm demure way, Tony responds,

"I'm very anxious; I just want this case to be over. To be concluded!"

"Bene! I understand." Portari reacts.

Tony settles quietly into the large soft leather chair across from the Inspector.

"Here are all my notes. I hope they can be of help to you."

The concerned Inspector replies with kindness.

"Tony, you have not only been a delight to work with, but you have been extremely useful. You must have been a damn good detective in NYC."

They both smile, while Tony grins.

Tony adds "I'm going across the street to the Museo di Buon Consilgio; I want to see how Dottore Franzoi is preparing for his *valuable artifacts* crates."

He turns and looks solidly at Portari, "See you after dinner for our larger plan."

With a tight smile, Tony dashes out the back door.

CHAPTER THIRTY-SIX

Walking across the cobblestone street, Tony goes north about a half a block to the Museo di Buon Consiglio. Pulling on its brass handle of the museum's massive wooden doors, he enters into the foyer, with its huge marble pillars and high Roman arched ceiling. As his eyes gaze around, he walks to the director's weighty highly polished mahogany door. The golden foiled engraved sign on this door declares:

DOTTORE CLAUDIO FRANZOI, DIRETTORE

Tony knocks. The door is opened by a smiling middle-aged tall man with grayish hair, and is sporting a well trimmed white mustache. He's dressed elegantly in a double breasted grey suit.

"Come in! Come va ? How are you doing?" speaking enthusiastically, as the director recognizes him and exclaims, "I'm so glad to see you!"

Tony accepts his pleasantries, because he knows that he has a high regard for his Zia Erna and her hotel.

The director points to a chair, "Si accomodi, I'm sorry

for the problems that your aunt is having. She has done a superb job with the hotel; I hope this tragedy gets resolved soon."

Tony sits, "Grazie!" Comfortably he begins asking,

"How are all your arrangements for the Florentine artifacts going?"

Dottore Franzoi, eagerly answers, "I'm very excited about the receiving of such valuable antique treasures from the Uffizi Galleria of Firenze, of course on loan. We're very busy getting ready for this year's Christmas Show."

He continues, "Roberto has been a tremendous help in making all the arrangements. He is in charge of securing the financial and the insurance applications which are required protection for these precious artifacts."

Tony smiles quietly. (He wonders if one of these men or both are involved in II Bel Fior Hotel's stolen da Vinci masterpiece mystery.)

Dottore Franzoi appreciatively adds, "I'm so grateful to Ispettore Portari for the placement of his carabinieri to protect these artifacts."

Tony gets up from his chair, "I wish you a successful show. I must go shopping, as I am leaving this week for my home in NYC."

Dottore Franzoi extends his hand, "Visit us soon again." Both smile.

Tony exits the museum. He proceeds to the Trento University legal library in search of some statutes.

After an hour of reading, he heads out in search of children's gift stores to buy toys for his niece and nephew. After purchasing a Barbie doll and an airplane, his eyes spot a jewelry store. He enters and buys two golden chained bracelets, one for his Mom, the other for his sister Gina.

Tony feels satisfied, as he examines his gifts. He walked

to the back of the carabinieri's office and places these gifts into his car's back trunk.

Suddenly and rapidly, Tony's gaze turns to the road across the street towards the museum.

CHAPTER THIRTY-SEVEN

Tony catches sight of the Inspector who's rushing across the street to the Museo di Buon Consiglio. A large van is parked in front of the museum. Inspector Portari and Dottore Franzoi are protectively watching the handling of these two precious crates. Each one focuses on the crates for their own different purpose.

The two crates are taken out of the canvas covered truck and are placed on rolling carts. The Florentine police officers escort and push the carts with the crates on to the freight elevator. As the elevator descends to the basement Arts room, the police agents roll the two crates to the corner of the basement Arts room; close the door and leave.

While the Inspector and Dottore Franzoi return to the main floor of the museum, the carabinieri stay below outside the basement door to keep surveillance. The doctor shakes the Inspector's hand and thanks him. They both depart.

Dottore Franzoi goes to the lobby to lock up the museum, while the Inspector goes back to his men to supply them with precise instructions.

Dottore Franzoi looks for Roberto to review the paperwork needed for the loaned artifacts insurance arrangements. He finds Roberto. They examine the insurance protection policy, they both agree positively.

It's after 5:00pm. The director and Roberto take their briefcases and punch in the security alarm codes. They cordially nod to each other. The museum is locked up.

While in the darkness of the basement, the two Florentine officers expertly emerge from their respective crate. They look around cautiously, and examine the Arts basement room. They immediately scamper to unbolt the grand heavy metal door of the Arts basement room. This polizia door plan provides the access for the carbinieri and the Inspector to enter the Arts basement room for the probable arrest of the criminals, involved in the horrendous plot and crimes surrounding the theft of the de' Medici's family owned, da Vinci masterpiece, the smaller "Annunciation."

With the Florentine polizia assignment accomplished, the two officers go back again to their designated crate to wait for the planned drama to unfold.

CHAPTER THIRTY-EIGHT

Tony has some time to get a quick dinner. He sees a quaint trattoria, La Giardiniera with an outdoor cafe.

His mind decides, "Hmm, I'll try this place for a relaxing meal,"

Tony places his order of pasta Bolognese and a coke with the young teenage waiter.

"No wine tonight! I need to be sharp." He says to himself glumly.

After his meal he strolls to his car and retrieves his black jogging suit from his auto's trunk. He saunters into the carabinieri's lavatory to change his clothes. He packs his morning outfit and returns them to his car's trunk.

Suddenly looking down at his wrist watch, he discovers that it's past seven in the evening. Tony realizes that he must hurry to Portari's office.

The carabinieri and Inspector Portari are already there.

Tony swiftly sits down to listen to all of the Inspector's instructions.

Portari stands in his casual dark jogging suit and vocalizes all his orders for this night's mission.

"Tony and I will be hidden in the outside corner of

the Arts basement door. Fausto and Carlo," he points to his officers, "You two will stay on either side of this metal basement door."

The Inspector continues, "The rest of you will spread out and surround the areas around the museum's property."

Portari stops and looks seriously at Tony.

"Tony! You are not to carry any type of gun. Although you are a great asset to me, I'm requesting that you stay in the background, behind me."

Tony nods and replies with great esteem of the Inspector. "Understood."

Continuing with his instructions, Portari orders "After the Florentine officers come out of their crates to arrest the alleged criminals, the carabinieri at the side of the Arts basement door will enter first.

Then the rest of us who are outside the basement's door will follow to assist the police officers with the arrest."

Finishing up with all the arrangements, the carabinieri leave to change into the dark athletic suits. The assigned officers disperse to their designated positions around the museum.

After a long review and discussion by Portari with Tony, they both leave the building. They look up and down the street, and cautiously proceed to the Museo di Buon Consilgio.

CHAPTER THIRTY-NINE

It is getting close to nine in the evening. The streets are silent and dark. All the stores are closed; even the awnings are rolled up. The 19th century styled hanging night lights show the only sign of life in their evening in Trento. The merchants have elected to close all the businesses every Monday at 7:00 pm for their evening off.

"What a perfect day to have the crates delivered," the Inspector deduces.

Tony and the Inspector cross the street. Everything is deserted and they see only their shadows on the ground. Wearing their rubber soled sneakers, they descend to the corner iron grilled window near the Arts basement door. They crouch in fetal position into the dark confined space near the window. Both stay quietly anticipating the drama that is about to unravel.

It's a little after 9:30 this evening when they hear a car park above them. They put their ears close to hear the activities. The museum door opens. No alarm goes off!

Portari surmises, "It must be either Dottore Franzoi or Roberto as they are the only two people who know the code to the alarm."

Suddenly they hear the freight elevator moving closer to the basement room. The door opens. Portari squashes his face to the window to see who it is. The light is flicked on.

"It's a young man. It's Roberto!" sotto voce the Inspector utters. (Portari puts his finger to his lips.)

Roberto opens the side vault and pulls out a large black leather briefcase. He lays it on the long marble table in the middle of the room. With the light dangling on a chain above the table, Roberto takes a careful look at the picture that he pulled out of the briefcase. He stares at the framed painting for a long time.

Outside the portal, Portari cannot see his expression.

"Could it be the stolen da Vinci masterpiece?" he wonders.

Securing the painting back into the briefcase, Roberto places it into the wall safe. He turns off the lights and proceeds to the elevator, up to the main floor.

Portari puts his finger to his lips, signaling to Tony to remain silent.

Then, Portari places his hand to his head, "What is Roberto doing now? Is he waiting for someone?"

After fifteen minutes pass, they hear another car above them arriving in the parking lot. They both try attentively to hear voices. They can't hear anything.

Another ten minutes elapse. They hear the brakes of a third vehicle arriving. Once more they hear the elevator descending down to the basement Arts room. Tony and the Inspector hear feminine voices. They are speaking rapidly as they come off of the elevator into the Arts basement room.

In the darkened corner of the basement room the Florentine polizia in the crates await for the unlawful planned transactions. They are positioned like crouching cats ready to pounce out of the crates to confront their alleged criminals.

The group from the elevator enters the Arts basement room where the hanging light is flicked on. Portari, still crouched by the window pane, can see Roberto with three women. He presses firmly to the window trying tenaciously to recognize the women.

Suddenly he gasps. "It's Gabriella," in a subdued tone.

"Damn!" Tony angrily jumps up. Portari pushes him down and puts his hand over his mouth. "Cool it" he says in a muted voice.

Roberto takes the briefcase out of the wall safe; he shows the painting to the women. Immediately he retrieves the painting from the woman and returns the framed painting back into the safe's vault.

The women sit stiffly, at attention, as if they are waiting for the fireworks to go off.

CHAPTER FORTY

As soon as Roberto secures the painting back into the wall safe, he leaves the women in the basement Arts room. He takes the elevator up to the main floor.

Portari and his staff anxiously wait for the larger plan to unfurl. Time passes at a snail's pace.

After fifteen minute pass. A fourth car is heard stopping in the museum's parking lot. Quickly the museum door opens; Roberto and his newly arrived guests go to the elevator. The lift is heard descending down to the basement Arts floor. This time male voices are heard from the elevator, stopping at the basement's Arts room.

One more time, Portari squeezes his face against the window pane, he sees two men dressed in black jogging suits. One of the men is carrying a silver metal briefcase.

Roberto gestures to the men to sit at the Arts marble table. Two of the women move to give the men center seats. Roberto removes the briefcase from the side wall safe; opens the case and pulls out the framed painting. The two new arrivals take out a portfolio of small instruments and spread them on the table. Not a sound is heard.

The men put on white cotton gloves. With intense

precision they begin their process of examining the painting thoroughly through the use of their small electronic microscope.

Continuing to press his eyes against the window pane, Portari observes these two males are continually examining the painting, first frontwards, then backwards. Roberto is scrupulously watching his guests, while the women are immobilized like stone statues at the end of the table.

As Roberto starts to take out a cigarette, one of the examiners puts up his fingers and violently shakes his head, as a NO!

Roberto sits down, bends his head low. The examination of the painting takes about twenty minutes. The men remove their gloves and place the framed painting gently into its green felt folder, to be nestled back into the black leather briefcase.

Roberto jumps up. He seems happy.

The deal is a go! The silver metal case is opened, exposing large stacks of euros.

Roberto, with the women hovering close by his side, reviews the count of the euros. He closes the case and Roberto shakes the men's hands.

"It's a deal!" Portari whispers.

Unnoticed the Florentine policemen spring out of their crates, shouting "Polizia! Polizia!

You're under arrest; put your hands up into the air, above your heads."

CHAPTER FORTY-ONE

The heavy basement door springs open. The Inspector, the carabinieri and Tony storm into the basement Arts room. All, but Tony have their revolvers drawn. Tony stays in the background, behind Portari.

Inspector Portari strongly announces "You're all under arrest for the felony murder of Signora Louisa de' Medici and the theft of her da Vinci masterpiece."

Mirella starts screaming and jumping at her mother, Bruna D'Amici, "What have you done to me!

Mama, per piacere, help me?"

Bruna looks sternly at Mirella "Be quiet, they're only guessing."

With all the activities in progress, quietly Gabriella leans down out of sight, and sneakily puts her hand into her hip pocket.

Inspector Portari with his quick eye on the situation, unsparingly shouts at Gabriella,

"Stand aside, don't you dare reach for anything, put your hands high up above you, where I can see them."

"No! No, Ispettore Portari," quickly the Florentine policemen step forward.

"She's one of us, she is our undercover officer. She has been working on this case since Signora de' Medici announced her loan of her masterpiece to this Trentino museum."

They gaze at her with surprise. Mostly, Tony looks at Gabriella with joyous relief. His heart jumps, as he smiles at her.

"Why didn't you tell us, we could have helped you?" As Tony puts his hand on her shoulder.

"It would have blown my cover," she responds vindicating herself.

Signora D'Amici screeches at Gabriella in a bitchy demeanor and an acerbic tongue. "Tradittora! You used us."

"No, I was only doing my job," Gabriella proudly defends herself.

Roberto vehemently tells the Inspector, "I had nothing to do with the murder."

Mirella continues sobbing, "I didn't do anything. I just accompanied my mother to the museum to pick up her ordered frame."

Portari declares, "You can call your lawyers at the police station."

The alleged criminals are handcuffed and taken to the carabinieri's jail house.

Inspector looks kindly at Gabriella, "I need all your paperwork."

"I'll come to your office, shortly."

Tony goes over to her side.

"After you are finished with your paperwork, I'll drive you to the hotel, you need a rest."

All she could answer is a soft "Grazie."

CHAPTER FORTY-TWO

It's after eleven pm that evening; all the alleged criminals were safely taken to the carabinieri's jailhouse.

Inspector Portari calls Dottore Franzoi immediately, to inform him of all that has transpired at the Museo di Buon Consilgio. As the director of the museum answers the call, Portari informs him that the de' Medici murder and the theft of her stolen masterpiece has been resolved this evening at his Trentino museum.

Doctor Franzoi replies surpricingly, "How did this all come about?"

Portari continues, "I need for you to go over to the museum tonight to assist my officers secure and close the museum. Much has occurred this evening, I need to take care of the three alleged criminals that were arrested this evening. I promise to relate all the information early tomorrow morning."

Doctor Franzoi answers, "I understand your immediate situation. I'll go directly to the museum and secure the place with the alarm system. I'll leave my questions to you, tomorrow in the early morning at my office."

*

Tony drives Gabriella to the police station, so that she can submit all her paperwork for this evening activity.

She turns to Inspector Portari, "I'll write up all my involvement from this evening, but I'll come tomorrow to release my complete notes on this case, after I have spoken to my superior Ispettore Odericci."

"That's fine." Portari nods in agreement. Ciao, see you tomorrow."

Portari walks over to Tony and quietly advises him, "I think you should prepare Angelica, as I'm going to the hotel late tomorrow morning to inform the hotel staff about this evening's development."

As Tony leaves the Inspector, he strides over to Gabriella; he takes her hand and leads her to his car.

"Your car is safely parked in the back of the carabinieri's building; I'll help you retrieve your vehicle tomorrow."

In his automobile Tony's smiling eyes look at Gabriella and kindly tell her, "I'm so glad that you're one of us, I thought I lost you."

As her eyes fill up with tears, she declares "Never! I thought my heart would break when you looked so severely at me."

"We'll talk more tomorrow in the morning." Gabriella closes her eyes peacefully in the moving car.

They arrive at II Bel Fior Hotel; Tony escorts Gabriella to her room. Although he aches to remain with her, he knows that she needs some sleep. He lets go of her hand and proceeds to kiss her on the lips.

His whole demeanor has been lifted, his heart and soul are delightfully roaring with happiness.

The only sadness remains with the job of telling Angelica about Roberto's involvement in the masterpiece's theft and murder of La Signora de' Medici.

"That's for tomorrow." He convinces himself. He goes to his room, puts on his pajamas and promptly falls on the bed, where he drifts into a tired, deep sleep.

CHAPTER FORTY-THREE

The church steeple is chiming seven bells!

As Tony is turning over in bed. He mutters to himself, "Just a little longer."

After ten minutes pass, Tony drags his body into the shower to get ready for his encounter with Zia Erna and Angelica. With well-protected determination and compassion, he wants to speak with Zia, first. He believes that she could lighten the burden of the Roberto fiasco for Angelica.

He crosses the street to Zia's house; Zia Erna appears on her apartment's terrace.

Anxiously, she ambles over to open the door to her kitchen.

"Come in, I've been worried about you. I feel something terrible is happening."

Zia hands Tony a cup of caffè latte. He pushes it away, dreading what he is about to say.

"Please sit down." As he gently puts his arm around his aunt, he leads her to a chair. Zia looks at Tony apprehensively. "What's happening?"

Tony answers, "The masterpiece has been recovered. Last night three criminals have been arrested."

Zia answers excitedly, "What's the matter? How does it affect us?"

"Zia please stay calm, I need you to help me comfort and support Angelica."

Zia anxiously shouts, "Ma perche? Please, tell me!"

Tony looks at his aunt, and says, "The alleged criminals are Bruna and Mirella D'Amici. And the third person arrested is Roberto!" Tony continues in a low voice,

"They were all arrested of the felony murder of Signora de' Medici and the theft of her da Vinci masterpiece." Zia falls to the side of her chair, gasping, then sobs.

She picks up her head and says, "How could that be?"

"How could that be? Oh, my poor Angelica!"

"Zia, please you must have courage," Tony pleads.

Zia looks into Tony's eyes, "Si, I will be strong and help you inform Angelica."

"The Inspector is coming to the hotel around 10 am to advise the staff regarding the conclusion of this horrible crime. Before he comes, I want to prepare Angelica." Tony pleads.

"Securo, let's go over to the hotel and comfort Angelica," Zia advises.

CHAPTER FORTY-FOUR

Tony and Zia Erna cross the street, where they swiftly enter the hotel's kitchen. It's a quarter after 8am. Angelica is cleaning and storing the fluted champagne glasses into their respective cases.

She looks up and smiles, "Ciao, Zia."

Then she speaks to Tony, "Come va?

How's everything going?"

Tony asks her to sit down. Angelica quickly responds, "What's the matter?

Zia looks so pale, did someone die?"

"No!" Tony exclaims. "But I must speak with you, please."

He insists, "Sit down."

"Okay!" Angelica sits between the two of them.

Tony commences, "The masterpiece has been recovered."

"That's great!" Angelica's eyes widen.

"Angelica, let me finish, the criminals have been apprehended. Inspector Portari has them in custody." Angelica looks confused.

"Mirella and her mother, Bruna D'Amici were arrested."

Tony keeps speaking, "And the other alleged suspect is------- Roberto!"

He's arrested for the theft of the de' Medici's masterpiece and the felony murder of La Signora de' Medici," Tony's voice tightens.

After a short silence of not comprehending, Angelica screeches, "O, my God!"

She puts her head on the table and sobs. Suddenly, she looks up at Zia, "How could this be?"

Zia takes her fondly in her arms. After a few minutes, Angelica lifts her head.

"I knew there was something wrong, because for the past six months Roberto has been distant with me, rarely did he kiss me. I thought he had a new girlfriend.

What will happen now? I feel so sorry for his mother."

Tony informs Angelica that the Inspector will visit the hotel at ten o'clock today to explain the situation of the arrests.

"You don't need to be present."

"That's considerate of you," through moistened eyes, she continues, "Tony, I thank you for your kindness, but I'm a survivor.

With all your love, I will come through this crisis.

But I'll pass on the meeting with the staff," She advises.

"I'll finish my work here, then, I'll go to my apartment."

Tony embraces Angelica, and then he leaves.

Zia Erna stays to help her with the packaging of the champagne glasses. She stays and caringly accompanies Angelica back to her apartment.

CHAPTER FORTY-FIVE

Meanwhile, in the early morning at the carabinieri post, Inspector Portari is preparing for his appointment with Dottore Franzoi and his interrogation of the three arrested criminals from last evening.

Portari picks up his telefonino and calls Inspector Odericci.

"Pronto, this is Ispettore Portari; I want to speak with Ispettore Odericci."

"Subito!" answers the officer on the other line.

Odericci replies, "Pronto, Portari, so glad to hear from you."

*

"Bene! I just wanted to update you regarding the de' Medici case. We especially want to thank your police officers for doing a great job. A special thanks to Sergente Gabriella Longhi for her splendid undercover work."

Odericci responds, "Si, we are so grateful. We will commend our officers, especially Sergente Longhi. It was a pleasure working with you and your staff. Regarding the ex-con men who assisted in the exposure and the attainment of the da Vinci's masterpiece, we have already given them an earlier parole. We will deal with them, while your judicial system will prosecute the three arrested criminals. If you need any of my officers for your court case, call me and I will gladly assist you. Ciao, best of everything to you and your carabinieri."

Portari reacts, "That sounds fine, by the way I informed Professore Leonetti that the de' Medici stolen masterpiece is under police protection and security. After the court sentencing of these three alleged criminals is completed, the da Vinci painting will be returned to him. Grazie for all the help from you and your professional department. Ciao! WELL DONE."

Portari puts down his telefonino and leaves for his appointment with Dottore Franzoi.

Portari grabs his wool jacket and leaves for his appointment at the Museo di Buon Consiglio.

He crosses over to the other side of the street to the museum. As the Inspector reaches the top of the stairs, he pulls on to the huge brass handles and enters the museum. Portari knocks on the director's door.

Doctor Franzoi opens the door and amicably asks Inspector Portari to enter. The director points to a chair, "Si accomodi."

Portari informs the director, "I've come to explain what has occurred at this museum last night."

The director listens attentively.

"Last week, the Trentino carabinieri and the Florentine polizia were informed that the de' Medici's stolen masterpiece, da Vinci Annunciation, was up for sale at your museum last evening. The two police agencies concocted a plan to surprise and apprehend the alleged criminals of their crimes."

Portari continues, "We set up a plan to change your two crates of artifacts for two police officers. *You never received any artifact* but, in Firenze their officers were placed into two aerated crates to be delivered to your Arts basement room. After all the participants of this crime arrived, the two Florentine officers came out to arrest these alleged criminals. My police officers and I completed the arrests. We attained and secured La Signora de' Medici's stolen masterpiece, the smaller "Annunciation" by da Vinci."

Dottore Franzoi responds, "Wow! And who are the arrested criminals?"

"The three criminals are Bruna and Mirella D'Amici," and quietly he utters, "Roberto Scoffo."

The director sits still in shock. "Well I don't know what to say."

Portari advises,

"Now you can arrange with the Uffizi galleria in Firenze for your replacement artifacts."

"I'll take care of the replacements for our Christmas Art show," The director reassures.

The director thanks the Inspector Portari. They both shake hands and Portari takes off for the prison, to do his interrogation of the three arrested criminals of last evening.

CHAPTER FORTY-SIX

At the prison, Portari walks into an austere high white walled interrogation room. Mirella sits at the bare small table, wearing her orange untied prison uniform. Her long hair is loosely unmanaged falling over her face, as she looks at Portari. He views her red puffy eyes. By her side sits Paolo Rossi, her lawyer.

She screeches tearfully, "I didn't kill La Signora de' Medici!"

Her attorney attempts to calm her down.

"Okay, don't say anything."

Signor Rossi states, "Mirella would like to speak with the head of the magistrate's office.

She will cooperate and wants to plead her case."

"Bene! I will arrange for a meeting with magistrate's office," responds Inspector Portari.

The lawyer looks up to Portari, "By the way I'm also representing Roberto Scoffo and Bruna D'Amici. Roberto wants to see the magistrate, also."

Portari calls on his telefonino to bring Roberto Scoffo into the room.

Roberto enters the room in his baggy orange prison

suit. His mood is pleasant, as he pleads, "I only helped Signora D'Amici with the disposition of the masterpiece. I will cooperate with this case.

Per piacere! I want to plea bargain these severe charges," intensely he speaks.

Looking at Mr. Rossi, the lawyer, Inspector Portari asks,

"What about Bruna D'Amici?"

"No, she wants to speak with you."

Inspector calls his prison guards into the room.

"Take these two prisoners back to their cells, and bring Bruna D'Amici back to this interrogation room."

Bruna arrives in the room. Her face is acutely taut as she glares at Portari. Her hair is severely pulled back into a bun. She stands erectly in front of the small table dressed in her orange prison garb.

Portari demands, "PLEASE! Sit down."

She sits across from the Inspector, saying in a cutting edge tone and shrilling harshly,

"You have nothing on me!"

Inspector Portari slightly smiles on the side of his face,

"I believe we have a very good witness in Gabriella Longhi."

Bruna smirks.

The Inspector stares at Bruna, "By the way, your daughter and Roberto are willing to confess to their crimes, in order to cop a plea deal.

What do you think of that?"

Bruna's face hardens; it becomes scarlet red in color, it appears like it's bursting with anger. She swirls to her attorney, and then Mr. Rossi states that he needs time to speak with his client, privately.

"Bene, I have to go out, you take your client back to her cell and let me know the outcome."

Portari calls for her female guard. Mr. Rossi and Bruna leave for their discussion in her cell.

The Inspector grabs his heavy jacket and takes off for II Bel Fior Hotel.

CHAPTER FORTY-SEVEN

Portari arrives at the hotel in the late morning, where he asks Marco to assemble his staff into the small dining room. Marco informs the Inspector that all the guests are leaving for their homes today.

"Good, I don't need them," answers Portari.

Inspector thanks all the workers for their cooperation and patience.

"I want to tell you that the case has been solved. The masterpiece has been recovered."

They all look delighted. The Inspector firmly continues, "But there is further information that I want to impart to you. We've arrested three alleged criminals."

Mirro asks brusquely, "And who are they?"

"This is going to be difficult for you. We arrested Roberto Scoffo." There's a loud collective gasp.

They look around for Angelica. Not seeing her there, they surmise that she already knows.

Inspector seriously carries on, "The other two arrested persons are: Bruna D'Amici and her daughter Mirella."

Mirro quickly breaks from the group and runs out of the hotel. Zia is feeling the sting of her nephew's pain. She rushes out of the hotel, to her relatives' apartments, to give comfort to her niece and nephew.

Portari continues, "The hotel must NOT be restored until the criminals are brought to justice. I will notify you when you can redo the hotel." His eyes look at Marco.

Speaking for his aunt and the hotel workers, Tony steps forward, he fondly expresses his gratitude to Portari for a job well done. Tony shakes his hand and pats him on the shoulder. The Inspector then takes his leave.

Tony announces to his relatives, "I'm leaving Friday for NYC. I love you all, but I must get back to NYC." They surround him with hugs and gratitude for all his help.

Marco says to the staff, "Bene, let's finish our straightening of this hotel." They all disperse, and continue with their assigned hotel tasks.

Tony goes to his room and calls his mother to inform her that he will arrive at JF Kennedy Airport, this Friday at 3:30 pm.

Then he phones Gabriella to notify her that he is ready to assist her in retrieving her vehicle in Trento.

Gabriella hurries to Tony's room, they both embrace and kiss. Since they are both pressed for time, they leave immediately for Trento. On the trip, Gabriella tells Tony that she is taking her aunt back to Firenze, today.

Tony answers, "Good! I want to bring you up to date; I'm leaving this Friday for NYC."

There's a silence. Gabriella sweetly responds, "I'm sorry you're leaving so soon, I'll come to see you off at the airport.

Just tell me what airline and at what time?" Gabriella asks.

Tony smiles. He affectionately replies, "Marco Polo Venice Airport, Friday at 3 pm – with Delta Airline."

"I'll be there," Gabriella lovingly answers.

CHAPTER FORTY-EIGHT

Portari arrives at his office to find a message from Mr. Rossi. He quickly calls the lawyer. Mr. Rossi advises the Inspector that he gave Mirella and Roberto's confessions with their pleas to the magistrate's court.

He continues "Now Bruna D' Amici feels that she wants to tape her confession, it's the only way she can save her daughter."

The Inspector pensively responds, "Come to my office late this afternoon, to complete her case."

The attorney declares, "How's four pm this afternoon?"

"Fine!" answers Portari.

Mr. Rossi shows up promptly for his appointment to assist his client. The officer at the door swiftly telephones the Inspector. After a few minutes, Portari strides out to greet the lawyer. They both shake hands, and Portari arranges for the guard to bring Bruna D' Amici into the interrogation room.

Bruna comes into the room looking tired and her posture is slumped over. She has lost her brash outward personality.

Portari sits across the table from Bruna and her counselor, unwaveringly saying,

"Are you ready to make your statement, truthfully?"

"Si!" Signora D'Amici answers slowly.

The Inspector looks at Bruna's lawyer, Mr. Rossi. He asks permission to tape their conversation.

Mr. Rossi answers, "Si."

Portari stands forthrightly, in front of Bruna D'Amici.

"Why have you changed your mind?"

"My daughter had nothing to do with the plan of stealing La Signora de' Medici's painting. The only thing she has confessed to are the petty thefts which occurred at the II Bel Fior Hotel. She needed money for her University studies. She had nothing to do with La Signora's murder."

The Inspector looks doubtfully, "Didn't your daughter leave the Signora de' Medici's door open for you to get in?"

"No! I sneaked into the room when the waiters were delivering the La Signora's luggage to her hotel room."

Portari plants his foot on the stool. "Wasn't your daughter arrested at the museum, last night?"

Bruna shrills, "Si, but she didn't know of my plans. I asked her to come to help me pick up my ordered frame at the museum. I did not want her in on the plan. Roberto will attest to this fact. I should have never taken her with me."

Portari looks suspiciously at his prisoner. "You certainly know how to cover for your daughter.

Tell me, who was waiting for the painting that you dropped from La Signora de' Medici's window?"

"Roberto!" Bruna answers.

"Let's proceed to the night of the robbery of the masterpiece and Signora's de' Medici's assault. Were you in the room?"

"Si!" Bruna responds.

"By yourself? " She answers quietly, "Si!"

Portari continues determinedly, "We're you a friend of La Signora de' Medici?"

Again, Bruna replies, "Si!"

The Inspector looks fiercely at his prisoner. "Did you hit Louisa de' Medici on her head with the marble statue of Julius Caesar?"

Bruna hesitates.

"Did you hear me?" Portari shouts loudly.

Bruna begins to sob. Her lips are trembling, "I didn't want to harm her or kill her, and I just wanted her masterpiece. She had so much."

Again, Portari loudly repeats

"Did you hit La Signora de' Medici on the head with the marble bust of Julius Caesar?"

"Si, si! I didn't want to harm her, she was my friend," She screams.

Portari stares disgustingly at Bruna, "Et tu Brute!"

He continues loudly, "You hit her with the marble bust of JULIUS CAESAR!" She sobs fiercely and intensely, "Si!"

Portari stops for a few minutes, allowing her, the confessed murderer to compose herself.

"I believe you have helped your daughter." Looking at her lawyer, Portari states that he will send all her tapes and written confession to the magistrate of Trento. Also, he will give Mr. Rossi a copy of all these items.

Portari continues, "Signor Rossi, the judicial system of Trento will advise you of the sentencing date. Grazie, everything is completed. I'll see you then."

Mr. Rossi requests that he look over the tapes and the final papers before they're sent to the magistrate. The Inspector agrees and will comply with his request.

Portari calls for the guard to escort Mr. Rossi and Bruna back to her prison cell.

Alone, the Inspector takes a deep breath. "It's over!"

His mind reflects, (when the case is brought to justice, then I will notify all of the involved parties of the results.)

CHAPTER FORTY-NINE

Friday arrives and Tony goes to Zia's apartment to have breakfast with his aunt and Angelica. He sits comfortably with them, talking about all his plans and items that he has to attend to in NYC.

Looking at Angelica with concern, "How's it going?"

"I'm keeping myself busy, but I did go to see Roberto's mother. She told me that Roberto is plea bargaining his case. He requested that I don't visit him."

Tony affirms, "Justice must be served!"

All of a sudden the four brothers and their families come strolling into Zia's kitchen.

"Ciao, Tony, we came to thank you for all your help, during the hotel tragedy."

Marco expresses their gratitude on behalf of the hotel staff, by handing him a gift of a sculptured angelic statue. This statue is one of the artistic images from the collection of the Contessa di Thun, a treasure from the Trentino-Tyrolean region of Italy.

"Grazie!" Tony warmly accepts.

Cheerfully, the group beseeches Tony, "You must return, this time on a well deserved vacation."

"Grazie, I'll certainly do that." He looks at his watch, "I must go to the airport. Thanks again! (Smilingly), see you soon when the hotel re-opens."

Tony enters his rental car, and travels to Venice Airport. Arriving at the airport, he returns his vehicle and then proceeds to get his boarding pass.

He sits at his terminal anxiously waiting for Gabriella. After a short time, he sees a classy lady in a royal blue linen suit. As Gabriella hurries to his side, Tony catches a breathless view of this woman. His heart races at the sight of his love. He reaches out to embrace Gabriella, lifting her off the ground. Her face unveils a smile that could light up the Eiffel Tower.

Standing by her side, he quickly hugs and kisses her tenderly. Affectionately he takes her hand and leads her to take a seat. Tony has about an hour before his flight departs. They sit and continually make plans.

Tony requests, "You must come, soon to NYC on a vacation!"

Gabriella tells him, "I have much time coming to me. Darling, I will come soon; we will have ample time alone." Tony leans over and kisses her again.

The loud speaker announces that the Delta Flight to JFKennedy, New York is boarding. Once more Tony and Gabriella embrace and kiss. Tony picks up his backpack and proceeds to his gate, with his face continually looking back at Gabriella.

Gabriella stares out the wide windows waiting for the plane to depart. Her eyes fill with moisture. She stays there until the plane is away into the skies.

Gabriella whispers,

"Darling I'll see you, very soon." She slowly walks away.

EPILOGUE
(Fourteen Months later)
the following year

It's the beginning of November, II Bel Fior Hotel is preparing for its Christmas re-opening. Zia Erna is holding a huge amount of invitations to be sent out to relatives, friends, past clients and the community for their grand opening. After Zia posts her invites, she goes to the local trattoria to have a cup of caffè latte and a sweet roll; sitting at a small round café table, she reflects on the past year.

The most important item completed, is the disposition of Louisa de' Medici's murder case. The sentencing of the three criminals occurred in April of this present year. The Leonetti family was present. Also Inspectors Ordericci and Portari were on hand. Zia Erna was the only one asked by the Leonetti family to attend the sentencing. A limited press was admitted. The proceedings were opened to the public, but were limited due to small area of the court room.

Sipping her caffè latte, Zia Erna recalls the court's sentencing, she can still hear the strong voice of Judge

Capobianco asking the three charged criminals to stand and hear his decision.

"In accordance to your voluntary decision to confess to your crimes, and your request to plea vocally and in written form, that you are ready and willing to accept a plea deal. Due to these facts, no trial is required or necessary."

The judge looks at their attorney, "Mr. Rossi, any more requests or statements?"

"No, your honor," Mr. Rossi, their attorney declares quietly.

Judge proclaims in a determined voice: "I have examined all the documents, your statements, your confessions, your tapes, all the evidence, and the police reports. I hereby declare in the name of the Justice Department of Trento, Italy, I hereby declare the sentences of these three charged criminals."

"Please stand. I state publicly in front of this court in the province of Trento, Italy the sentences of these following confessed criminals:"

"Mirella D'Amici is charged with petty and grand theft of items stolen from II Bel Fior Hotel; she is sentenced to 3 to 5 years in prison." Mirella begins to sob.

The judge continues, "Due to the testimony and statements made by police officer Gabriella Longhi and Roberto Scoffo, which eliminated Mirella D'Amici from having any part in the felony murder of Signora de' Medici and the theft of the da Vinci masterpiece, the court dropped those charges against her."

The judge turns to Roberto Scoffo:

"Robert Scoffo for second degree felony murder and the theft of the da Vinci masterpiece; due to the collaboration and cooperation in apprehending the master of this crime, Roberto Scoffo will receive 12 to 15 years in prison."

Roberto lowers his head but he still hears a female who's sobbing in the back of the court. He knows it's his mother.

The judge stares at Bruna D'Amici:

"Bruna D'Amici for first degree felony murder of Louisa de' Medici and the grand theft of the da Vinci painting, the smaller "Annunciation", and for her cold hearted planning of these crimes, the court gives her 25years to life."

She stands stoically, without reaction.

They are all remanded to their respective guards to begin their prison sentences.

The judge calls the Leonetti family to the bench, "It's with great honor, that we return your valuable painting. Do you have provisions for the security of the da Vinci masterpiece?"

"Si," answers Luigi Leonetti, the Professore's son. "We have decided to loan it to the Uffizi Galleria for a while, until we can arrange its tour throughout Italy.

The masterpiece is insured and bonded."

"Well done, bene. We will give it over to your security guards for its travel to Firenze's Uffizi Galleria." The judge pounds the gavel on his desk.

THIS CASE IS CLOSED

After the sentencing, Zia continues to think back on how she asked Inspector Portari to call Marco, II Bel Fior Hotel's manager. Respectfully, he immediately telephones Marco regarding the outcome of the sentencing.

"Pronto, Signor Zini, it's Ispettore Portari, I'm calling to inform you that de' Medici case has been brought to justice. Your Zia will provide you with the details.

You can now restore the hotel, do whatever you want with the crime room."

Marco answers, "Grazie, thank you for calling me right

away. I will set up a meeting with Zia Erna and the staff to decide on a plan for the room and the hotel."

The next day, Zia Erna recalls the meeting in which she and her relatives decide to break open the crime room and the walls to construct a large sitting room, where large wide window panes would encircle the entire clientele's new reading room. Zia Erna arranged to furnish this area with an Italian provincial cherry wood settee and two leather arm chairs. Also in the corners of this expansive room she provided two small tables for arts and crafts projects for the visiting children. The plan for this sitting room was proposed that it will be adorned with seasonal flowers all year long.

The plaque on the room's entrance door will be engraved in gold leaf lettering:

LOUISA de' MEDICI'S SITTING ROOM

They all enthusiastically agreed. Moreover, Zia recalls her telephone call to Professore Leonetti advising him of this project. Her mind remembers his words.

"Grazie, my family and I are so honored by the naming, this sitting room after our beloved Louisa, we will come up to your hotel at your re-opening."

The carpenters and all the construction crew started their work immediately. The chamber was finished in two months with the sunshine blessing the room with joy and solace.

Zia Erna reminisces on how she looked at the newly placed gold foil plaque. Her eyes moistened as she looked upward,

"God bless you, Louisa."

The workers continued with the addition of an elevator in the back of the hotel for the elderly and the handicapped. Also they white washed all the rooms in the hotel to give the hotel a fresh look. The project was completed by

November. The staff was excited to start a new season, a new beginning.

Zia recollects the scene of calling for a meeting of her four nephews and Angelica, her niece, to disclose her retirement.

Zia spoke to them with loving admiration, "I want you to know that I appreciate all your efforts and support to me. I made a decision, I will retire this year and I have drawn up legal papers to make each of you a partner with me. We will all have equal shares. That's six shares."

Marco and Angelica exclaimed, "That's very generous of you!" They both hugged their aunt.

"You deserve it," Zia responded. The other brothers, even Mirro, had a smile on his face. They warmly advanced to thank their aunt.

Back at the trattoria, Zia Erna finishes her caffè latte, with a sigh. Her mind remains delighted with all her decisions.

PART TWO

The responses from the invitations are coming into the II Bel Fior Hotel as positive acceptance for the grand celebration. There is only one week left prior to the re-opening of their hotel. The hallways are decorated with large potted pink and red poinsettias. Each dining room table is arranged for six persons, stately displaying a golden laced table cloth with a small red potted poinsettia in the middle of each table.

In the corner of the large dining room, stands a ten foot freshly cut pine tree, staged with tiny glittering crystal light bulbs, sparkling in and out throughout every branch of this fragrant smelling Christmas tree. The hotel is elegantly ready for their guests.

The first to arrive on Wednesday is Tony and Gabriella. They rush to Zia Erna's apartment. Tony quickly embraces his aunt. She in turns reciprocates by embracing both Gabriella and Tony. Zia has been informed by her sister, Tony's mother, regarding the strong bond that developed between her nephew Tony and Gabriella.

Tony informs Zia, "Mama and my sister Gina will arrive tomorrow."

"Good, do they need any help?" Zia asks

"We'll pick them up from Venice Airport. We rented a car."

"Bene! By the way the Leonetti's are coming tomorrow, too."

They both leave to get settled in the hotel.

By Thursday, the hotel is filled to capacity. Finally, Friday arrives. The hotel completes all its preparations for their guests.

Bishop Carlo Martini comes to the hotel early Friday morning, to bless the Louisa de' Medici sitting room. The service is kept small and respectful with only the Leonetti family and the hotel staff present. The sun shines brightly, exhibiting the joys of this room to all in attendance.

They all retreat to get ready for the evening celebration at 7 pm.

The re-opening of II Bel Fior Hotel

That evening, Zia Erna with her silvery blonde braids coiffed around her head, stands by the opened front doors in her elegant Tyrolean white embroidered satin blouse and her ankle-length black velveteen shirt.

Enthusiastically, she welcomes each of her guests.

Next to her, Marco stands as straight as a soldier. In his finely tailored black tuxedo, he's ready to assist any guest. Throughout the dining room, Angelica in her slimming light blue silk gown is helping the guests with their dining arrangements.

At the dining room tables, the chefs, Zia's nephews, are dressed in their tailored black tuxedos; they're directing their waiters with the proper assistance for all of their guests. On the long white linen dressed tables, large silver platters display a plethora of hot meats of pork, veal and some assortment of cooked seafood.

In the center of the long table is an assortment of warm vegetables and cold salads. To compliment the other foods: risotto, polenta, and lasagna are served.

The guests gather throughout the hotel to enjoy and celebrate all the jubilant festivities.

Tony enters the dining room wearing a dark grey double breasted suit, while Gabriella follows and is attired in her soft emerald green velveteen gown. Arm in arm, they chicly ambulate into the grand dining room.

Angelica swiftly goes to her cousin. Angelica introduces Gabriella and Tony to her new friend.

"This is Stefano, my good friend."

"Piacere," They happily exchange greetings.

Gabriella and Tony are glad to see the sparkle return in Angelica's eyes. They also notice that Mirro has returned to his old self, telling his jokes again.

Tony and Gabriella circulate around the room. They begin speaking to the Montagni from the previous summer. Walking around the room, they sit for a short periods with many of the guests. While they're eating many delectable foods, they experience the pleasure of listening to the string quartet who is serenading the guests with soft classical music. The happiness in this room makes them enjoy leisurely, a couple of hours of good food and pleasurable music.

After Zia Erna attends to her guests in a gracious manner, she advances to the string quartet. She pleasantly asks for the use of their microphone. Zia stands in front of the guests,

"My staff and I gratefully thank you for attending this grand re-opening. There are a few pleasant items, I must report to you. First, I want to tell you that I'm retiring." The assembled guests gasp.

"I want to tell you that my nephews Marco, Mirro,

Gianni, Mario and my niece, Angelica, will take over the management of the hotel."

Marco steps in, "You can be assured that we will ask Zia for advice."

The guests applaud.

Zia Erna continues, "Today, Bishop Martini blessed the Louisa de'Medici sitting room. It's with great honor that we ask you to visit and use it. Professore Leonetti will speak with you, shortly."

"Next, it gives me great pleasure to announce the engagement of my nephew Tony and Gabriella. They plan to be married next spring." There was a loud roar of applause.

"After my talk we will celebrate their engagement with champagne and pastries.

Now it gives me great pleasure to present, Professore Luigi Leonetti."

The Professore stands affably, "I gratefully want to thank, Erna Zini,

Her staff and all of you, here present for the wonderful tribute to our Louisa, in remembering her memory with this marvelous sitting room."

"Tomorrow, at Santo Virgilio Cathedral in Trento, my family invites all of you to attend a Mass in Louisa's memory at eleven am. Bishop Martini and some Trentino priests will concelebrate this Mass. At the end of this Mass, we will respect Louisa's wishes, by loaning the da Vinci's small painting of the "The Annunciation" to Dottore Franzoi for their Christmas show at the Museo di Buon Consilgio."

The people stand up and gratefully applaud this gift. The Professore thanks the people by putting his hand by his heart.

The joyous celebration at the hotel continues till midnight.

PART THREE
Memorial Mass

It's Saturday morning, the winter sun is shining and the bells of Santo Virgilio Cathedral are majestically chiming for the grand memorial Mass for Louisa de' Medici. Bishop Carlo Martini and a few Trentino priests prepare for this joyous Mass. The Leonetti family and their relatives sit in the front pews. The church is overcrowded with the Trentino community families. Also, there's a large party of guests in attendance from II Bel Fior Hotel. The Inspectors Portari and Odericci and some of their police officers are present at the Mass. The press from the Art World is present.

Tony and Gabriella enter the side door of the cathedral. Seeing Inspector Portari, they both rush over to embrace him.

The Inspector enthusiastically evokes, "Benvenuti, Americani!"

Tony replies softly, bending his head close to his ear, "We'll see you after the Mass."

Tony and Gabriella walk down the aisle towards the back of the church. They gaze admiringly at the beautiful sunflowers which are tied to the end of each pew. But mostly they feel exhilarated by the delightful organ music which plays Mozart's "Ode to spring."

As the Bishop Carlo Martini concludes the Mass, he calls Professore Leonetti and his children to the altar. Continuing, he requests that Dottore Franzoi comes to the altar, too.

Professore Leonetti presents to Dottore Claudio Franzoi the loan of the masterpiece of da Vinci's small "Annunciation" for the Museo di Buon Consiglio upcoming Christmas Show.

Dottore Franzoi accepts the masterpiece, as it will be the first showing, on its tour around Italy. Emotionally, he clasps his hand together and places them over his heart.

"We are so very grateful; it will gloriously enhance our Christmas show."

He looks at Professore Leonetti, "I'm filled with large feelings, but all I can say, is "Mille grazie!"

Finally, Tony is sitting in the back rows of the church with Gabriella, his eyes light up with joy. At last he feels the satisfaction of his retirement from the N.Y.C. Police Department.

Tony takes Gabriella hand and locks into her eyes,

"It's finished!"

Gabriella face smiles broadly in agreement,

"Yes, it's completed ... but with a new beginning!"

CPSIA information can be obtained at www.ICGtesting.com
Printed in the USA
BVOW022342190212

283234BV00001B/1/P

9 781467 026208